A Protector's
Touch

OTHER BOOKS BY THE AUTHOR

The Alex Conner Chronicles
(Urban Fantasy/Supernatural Suspense)
Trust: The Alex Conner Chronicles Book One
Truth: The Alex Conner Chronicles Book Two
Forbidden: An Alex Conner Chronicles Novella
Only: The Alex Conner Chronicles Book Three

Eve of the Exceptionals
(YA Epic Fantasy)

The Dark Angel Series
(Dark Urban Fantasy)
A Darker Fall: A Dark Angel Novella

Jake the Growling Dog
(A Children's Picture Book about Kindness, Diversity,
& Friendship) under the pen name, Samantha Shannon.
Jakethegrowlingdog.com @jakethegrowlingdog

KEEP UP WITH PARKER SINCLAIR

Webpage: *www.parkersinclair.net*
Amazon Author Page: *https://www.amazon.com/Parker-Sinclair/e/B00Q33GTQM*
Facebook Fan Page: *www.facebook.com/ParkerSinclairbooks/*
Instagram: *@ParkerSinclairauthor*
Twitter: *@Parker_Sinclair*
Join my newsletter for free fantasy/Sci-Fi books:
http://eepurl.com/b9q07X

A Protector's Touch

Parker Sinclair

Rawlings Books, LLC

Rawlings Books, LLC
Visit our website at
http://RawlingsBooks.com

Edited by

Lia Fairchild & Amy Jackson
Cover Art by Jessica Ozment
Book formatting by Jessica Ozment

Mobi Edition ASN B07PVPTG4S
Paperback ISBN 978-0-9984053-9-1

To those who helped me find my way out.

Contents

Chapter 1

Covalent Bonds

Despite my best efforts using makeup that looked a little like cake batter, I'm positive everyone can still see the painful swirls of black and blue. I shouldn't have come onto campus, let alone shown up to the class we have together.

"I can't go in there—not today. Just look at me." I need to stop being afraid. But *he* told me not to come. Actually, it was more like an *or else* warning, but I'm sick of him and his threats. This time, he's gone too far. More like *off a cliff and into a black, suffocating abyss* too far.

"You can do this, April. Derrick needs to see that you aren't afraid of him anymore." Nia's sweet voice floats across the short distance between us as her dark, almond eyes blink at me through her glasses. "He can't keep you from living your life, and he definitely can't keep you from your classes. Plus, your dad will flip if your grades slip, and you know it."

Nia is right. I can't hide anymore. I didn't see anyone all weekend with this damn shiner, courtesy of my jerk of an ex-boyfriend, but it's Monday, and I can't miss this class. Being absent from chemistry before a lab day is academic suicide, and I am not letting Derrick get in the way of school, or my life, any longer.

"Do you need help with the door?" Yes, Nia and I are standing like two idiots blocking anyone else from getting into the theater-sized classroom for Organic Chemistry 201. Yet something else causes my skin to tingle, but I don't dare turn around. Instead, I grab Nia's arm and move out of the way with my head down.

"What the… Okay, don't pull my arm out of its socket. I'm coming. Oh, hi. Sorry. We're just waiting for someone. Oh, thank you. That's sweet."

Nia's tinkling voice floats toward the guy holding the door open for us like it's no big deal, but I can't even bear to look at him fully. I mean, not like this— okay, not ever. I've never been able to stare at much more than the back of his head or the broadness of his chest and shoulders. Occasionally I drift off, staring at his Lacrosse stick, because staring at his face or risking a meeting of our eyes was always too dangerous with Derrick in this class, no matter how many times I felt Shan Carp's eyes on me.

"April. Earth to April. He was just staring at you and you couldn't even—"

My arched eyebrows stop my good friend, and killer study partner, mid-sentence.

"You're right. I'm sorry. I know you don't want him to see it, but maybe he'd fight for your honor, you know, as in kick Derrick's ass for you. That jerk deserves it anyhow, and then you and Shan could live happily ever after."

Her back is to me now, but I can tell the kissy noises she's making, which serve as the soundtrack for her hands roving all over her back, are coming from her goofy mouth. She's smart as a whip and funny as hell. I keep her around for both.

"As hilarious as this all is, let's go before I lose my nerve." I let Nia lead, knowing she'll follow our plan of moving as far away from Derrick as possible in the upper back row. It's nice of her, considering we usually take a seat closer to the front—near Derrick—since she has a hard time seeing the board. I promised her I'd take good notes for the both of us.

I lean into her as we walk. "Damn it, Ida is here."

Ida's our lab teacher's assistant, and it looks like she's helping Professor Grady today. She always relies on Nia and me in lab, and she'll know right away that we're in an odd spot. Not to mention she's more brains than couth and will probably blast us in front of everyone for sitting so far away. She means well, but tact is not her forte.

"I've got us covered, don't worry," she whispers over her shoulder. "I texted her this morning—just in case. I told her you weren't feeling well and needed to keep away from everyone. She's so afraid of getting sick that she's the one who told me where we should sit."

"Do you ever miss a thing? I mean ever?"

It's not an exaggeration. Nia remembers stuff from when she was two, I swear. But she's like a gremlin at times. She cannot have more than one drink—or any drinks, for that matter: they go right to her head. Not to mention she also has to eat every two hours, or she gets the worst case of hangry I've ever seen.

My comment stops her. She spins around, with stick-straight hair floating and then resting perfectly to brush the tops of her shoulders as she smiles while pushing her glasses onto her nose, before continuing our trek toward our seat. I'm so envious, with my out-of-control curls that loathe straighteners, or hair dryers and brushes, for that matter. Ponytails are my usual MO, and a necessity as part of the cross-country team. I tell Nia it's practical; she says it's lazy. Well, she wakes up with hair like that, so I don't even want to hear it. Plus, I do primp. A little blush and mascara are more than some people do in college, thank you very much—especially those of us rolling into a 9:00 a.m. second-year chemistry class.

Staring at her back, I should have noticed when she stopped, but nope; instead, I smash my nose right into her shoulder, causing her to drop the bag with a loud thud. Our indecisiveness took so long that all eyes and bodies turned to us when my best friend's book-riddled bag crashed to the floor like a sack of rocks as Grady moved toward the podium.

Sinister laughter unleashes and my body tenses. It's Derrick and his buddy Chas. I don't even need to look over to confirm. Instead, I catch Nia's withering stare in a direction behind and below me before we take our seats with our eyes trained on the professor.

"Don't even give him a second to think he got to you. He's going to fail this class without you now anyhow, so maybe he'll just drop it eventually."

We both know that isn't going to happen. Derrick's one of the star soccer players. Coach Mac will get a harem of tutors to keep him eligible. I had just been convenient, and an idiot—a convenient idiot at that.

Thankfully, Ida walks toward my ex and his toady, shutting them up for good. She could be part giant, I swear. She's even taller than my six-five father and wider than some of the football players. As an exchange student from Germany, she's working her ass off on multiple degrees, hoping to have no problems securing a job and work visa.

Nia chuckles. "Chas is such a dimwit. I wish you could have seen the look on his face when Ida came over. He may have even peed himself." We both allow ourselves a well-deserved chuckle before settling in for a long and difficult lecture by Professor Grady.

I can't help my wandering mind at times; it's an insistent pondering as to why I let things get this bad with Derrick. It has been an ongoing debate between Nia and me. Why does love have to make us so blind and stupid? Having thought of myself as a smart and even-keeled girl, I never thought I'd find myself in an abusive relationship, but it happened. After finally reading the books on female empowerment sent my way by my aunt and joining a support group, I found a way to end it for good. I know I'm not alone on how easily it can happen. I am just feeling fortunate to have gotten out before some of the horrific things others shared in group became my reality. I touch my face mechanically and wince—well, almost lucky enough.

My zoning-out moment ends abruptly thanks to Nia's pencil jab in the arm.

"Do not space out on covalent bonds, please. We need good notes for this chapter. The textbook is crap."

She is right, and reading ahead, as usual. I can't wait for the rant about our textbook later. I think Nia's plan is to take over the world of textbooks someday. She's never met one she likes. Must suck to be smarter than the massive brains that came together to create the learning tool in the first place.

"It's okay. I'm on it. Don't worry." Someone stands up to my left, and I look up in time to see Shan leaving with his phone gripped tightly in his hand. It happens every so often, and I've spent time creating reasons for it while falling asleep mere yards away in my dorm room twin bed. Fantastical ideas lead me to concoct his life as a secret agent when he is called away on occasion for the safety of our country. My other thoughts weave a tale of him being a big brother, and when his sister needs him, he will drop anything for her in a heartbeat. Lastly, and the one I hope isn't true, is that the caller is his girlfriend. No, Shan doesn't seem the type to leave class over something as trivial as a needy girl. He's a good student and balances lacrosse and school. No, he wouldn't miss class for something that isn't urgent. Well, whatever it is, I've seen him talk to Grady from time to time, and I can tell they have an understanding; Grady even seems sympathetic. I hope it isn't something awful like an ailing parent. Even though I've never met his eyes, or spoken a word to him, I care about Shan and don't give it a second thought as I track his exit, hoping he'll return soon.

"Ha, Derrick, yeah suck it. She doesn't have eyes for you anymore," Chas hollers out despite Ida's previous warning. He may be Derrick's toady, but he doesn't miss a chance to rile him up—something that goes both ways.

Shit, I can feel Derrick's eyes burning into me without even seeing them for myself. He was always incredibly jealous, of everyone, which is complete crap since he's the one who cheated in our relationship. What they've said in group is true: they tend to control and unleash jealousy because they know what they've done, and if cheating was—is—easy for them, it must be for us, right?

Derrick doesn't know that I know about his other girls. I don't want to risk him hurting anyone else,

6

though I think the girl who told me is already scared of him, but she didn't want to keep it from me if it pushed me to leave him. Kim was her name, a first-year theater student. Her short red hair beautifully reflected off the moonlight at the soccer house. She was nearly shivering when she spoke to me.

"Derrick and I slept together," she said in a choked whisper while adjusting her collar and looking around.

The small bruises, Derrick's trademark, could be seen despite her best efforts. He called them love stamps, but that's not what they are. He likes to inflict pain, to mark someone as his for all to see. It's just another form of control with a stamp of violence.

If this had been the first five times I'd heard about Derrick's treachery, I would have felt hot tears burst away from my eyes at her words, but not this time.

"Are you okay, Kim?"

"Am I-I okay? How can you not be pissed?" she asked. "After he threatened me not to tell you, I could tell he was a total dick, and no one deserves a boyfriend like that."

"It's not the first time, and if I don't leave Derrick, it won't be the last, so thank you for telling me." I made a poignant look at her neck. "We're both better off without him. You know that, right?"

Kim was the one with the tears that time. Ones that flew away as she nodded vigorously.

"Don't make the same mistake I did. Those love marks on your neck are only the beginning, and they only lead to more pain."

I wish I had learned that sooner.

Minutes tick by before I hear the creak of the door opening again, and the footfalls I've grown to memorize as Shan's walk down the auditorium steps. I don't stare this time, only seeing him out of the corner of my eyes. His green T-shirt, snug to his chest, and his amazing hair are all I need to see, for now. I had him in my bio class when we were freshmen last year, and I used to wonder what his room looked like and if I could somehow run into him at a party, but I never did. I met Derrick instead.

I feel myself relax with him back, exhaling like I had been barely breathing since his exit. I know Derrick's looking again, and I don't care. Shan may not care or know that I exist, but he already helps me by just being around. People give off vibes, you know, and his are warm, strong, and caring. I've seen him help Tim with his wheelchair, Ida when she had difficulty pronouncing a word, and Jack when he falls asleep. At least he doesn't smack him awake like I've seen Derrick do to Chas. God, I'm glad Derrick and I don't have any other classes together.

"Enough already." Nia looks at me with squinting eyes.

"Sorry, pencil problems." More like mind problems. I'm barely even out of a relationship, a terrible one at that, and I'm pining over some guy in chem class. It's so cliché. He doesn't want—oh, what did Derrick call me each time I tried to leave him—damaged goods, baggage, a slut? Yes, all of those. I don't even think I know how to be with someone. Derrick played so many games that my mind and my body are too confused to think of anyone touching a single part of me for a long time.

Class ends and Nia snags my notes from the desktop. "These look good. I knew I didn't need to worry."

I shake my head at her, knowing she was in fact worried the whole time. She's a bit of a control freak with school, but that's her thing. School is her life. Hey, we all have our things. Mine are running and reading. I get lost in my mind when doing either.

"Let's just wait till everyone's gone. I doubt he's going to sit out there till we come out."

It hurts, deep in my chest. She saw things so clearly when I didn't. Derrick was my first love, my first everything. I was so busy in high school, and overprotected by my parents, that I did not have time to think about boys. Seeing it now, it was all wrong.

I don't know how I missed Shan talking to Professor Grady and Ida as they walked up the steps toward the exit, but before I know it, Ida is calling out to me with the biggest I-am-so-sorry smile on her face. Whatever she's just done, and with how well I know her, I know she has a good reason. I freeze in our row, not wanting to get too close for anyone to see the bruising on my face. Grady continues on, after she smiles and nods, while Ida and Shan look our way. My mouth goes crooked, as it does in every picture taken of me—I mean ever. Oh no, I must look like a crazy person standing back here, instead of moving forward, but I can't will my legs to move.

"Sorry to put you on the spot, April, but Professor Grady recommended that Shan borrow your notes from what he missed, seeing as you are the only ones here, and some of the best in the class, it has kind of just worked out that way, if you don't mind."

Well, shit. What am I going to do now? Plastering on a big smile, I look to Nia, who fumbles around before jumping in to my rescue, moving in front of me in a clumsy and sad leapfrog-like maneuver.

9

"Sure thing, Ida. I just need to borrow them for a little while, since I had a little trouble seeing some things back here, and then we can give them to, um, Shan is it?"

Not being able to stop myself, I look up directly at my crush. And there it is, the first locked-eyes moment between me and my object of affection from afar, Shan. A charming smile plays at his lips as he takes me in, being a gentleman, not tilting his head or moving his eyes much to look me up and down. I can still feel him on every part of me just the same. And then he stops, his smile leaves, and I can see his pupils dilate even from where I stand. He's seen it. I know he has, and he looks angry—or wait, is that disappointment? Whatever it is, he says something quickly to Ida before walking away. Away from me, away from my pathetic-looking face, the one that put up with Derrick's crap for way too long. I am damaged, and Shan isn't having any part of it, or me.

Chapter 2

Facing the Truth

Even Ida manages to make it out of the classroom before my feet can even move me past our row. Another pencil nudge from Nia, and I put one foot in front of the other to make my way toward the door before my fingers close around the handle.

"Well, that didn't go so bad." Nia takes one look at my bunched-up shoulders and sighs. "I mean, at least Derrick didn't act like his usual tool self. And look, you took great notes."

Merely shaking my head, I pull on the handle and slip into the warm, spring mountain air. The year is almost over, one that I managed to maintain academically but let fall apart personally. Next year will be better; hell, tomorrow will be better. It has to b—

My thoughts are invaded by a loud thud against the wall of the science building. I've heard that sound before. It's hardly the first time Derrick has tried to hit me, or someone else, with a soccer ball. The black and white ball is gone before my eyes can track it, the force causing it to ricochet back toward its owner while a nasally bystander laughs at our expense.

"Cut it out, Derrick. Can't you find someone else to stalk?"

I spin toward Nia, my eyes pleading with her to not egg him on. She may be tiny, but she's obviously done watching me shy away from my bully of an ex-boyfriend.

"The next one won't miss. Will it?"

I turn my eyes on Derrick, getting my glare in order before meeting his eyes. Why does he still have power over me, even from this distance, in broad daylight? Granted, most people have left this area, and he knew that. He managed to convince me to make out with him against this very wall after class.

"Nobody's looking, so stop being a prude," he'd jab, with a fake smile curling his lips. "You're ashamed of showing others you're with me, aren't you? I know you don't really love me."

Makes my skin convulse just thinking about it, about his hands on me, owning me, not loving me. His lips forcing themselves onto mine, outside for anyone to see, seems more like a statement of his bounty and pride than showing me tenderness. I can still feel his teeth on my neck, biting me and marking me. All of the motions on top of the vile words that caused just as much damage to my psyche.

"We get it, you can play with your ball, now leave us alone before I call for campus security." Nia takes out her phone and preps to hit the alert button on her app.

"It's okay. He was just leaving, weren't you, Derrick?"

The voice responding to Nia is somewhat familiar, but it takes me a minute to register it as Tim's before I turn to see him wheeling himself over, with Shan right

12

behind. This is humiliating, only adding to the damaged image I've already revealed to the guy I've been pining over.

Though Derrick knew an audience wasn't in his best interest, he was rarely one to care. His coach was in good with the dean of students, something he was sure to hold over me plenty of times. Even though he didn't care much for anyone but himself, he may have accepted Tim's words and backed off, even if for the purely "saving face" factor, yet once he saw Shan not far behind, someone he perceived as a threat to his claim over me, I could see his muscles bulge and expand within his patented soccer jersey, along with his anger.

"This is none of your business, stick boy." Derrick seethes, jerking his pointed finger in Shan's direction. "If you think you're getting into her pants by coming to her rescue, you've got it all wrong. She doesn't like pussy mamas' boys, and that's all you are, isn't it?" Derrick walks over to Tim and Shan, but his crony, Chas, stays spinelessly behind.

My body moves by an outside force as Nia grabs onto my arm and we come together like magnets, watching the three boys face off all because of me and my crazy ex. Thankfully, neither Tim nor Shan look at us as Derrick approaches; I couldn't bear to meet their eyes.

Shan remains silent, but Tim doesn't. "We're just stopping some good-ole-boy bullying at our college, man. No need to mess with these ladies, is there? I'm sure you have something better to do with your time, right Pelé?"

Tim is older, having been forced to leave for a couple years to regain his strength enough to return to

13

school after a horrible accident. He may never fully recover the use of his body, but that has no impact on his quick mind. Everyone knows he'll be in line for a TA position. Derrick would be crazy to mess with someone so beloved by the staff and students alike. His story made national news, bringing Crimson State to the spotlight as well, and Derrick can't live without his spotlight.

"My beef isn't with you, Tim. It's with your little friend behind you. Tell him to leave my girl alone and everything will be just fine."

"I'm not your girl, Derrick." I spit out his name and curse my damn jaw for allowing the words to escape. "Not anymore," I manage, in a reduced yet powerful whisper.

Now they are all looking at me, and though my first instinct is to disappear into the shadows, to shrink and shy way, I remember that's what got me here in the first place. I let Derrick rule our relationship and make me feel like I was at fault for his temper. I know better now, and he will never change. This last chance I gave him proved that to me, but I don't think he'll ever understand.

"You say that now, but you'll be back. You're predictable, April. You'll always come back."

I clamp my jaw down tight this time. There is nothing to say in response, and I am not getting into some quarrel with him in front of everyone. I don't want their pity or the shame I feel to overwhelm me in front of their eyes. I just want Derrick to leave, and with a wave of his hand meant to dismiss me, he clomps away.

14

"Sorry, guys. I didn't mean for you to get involved." There I go again, always apologizing. I'm supposed to be working on that. Supposed to be.

"What she means to say is, thank you." Nia's voice is strong yet soft. "Derrick's a jerk, and everyone knows it. You don't need to apologize for him, ever."

"No biggie, ladies. It's all part of the knight in shining armor thing I've got going on." Tim uses strong arms to move his shiny, silver wheelchair in all directions in his fashionable vest and slacks—dressed to the nines as always. "But I can't take all the credit. My man Shan here is the one that told me to hang back a minute. Guess his spidey-senses also pick up on damsels in distress. Not that you can't take care of yourself, I mean, not to discount women's strength, you know."

Though Tim stumbles over his last few words, Nia and I are both smiling at him. I'm even managing to hold my own when his eyes land on my bruise.

I need better makeup.

Nia's finger-poke into my side causes me to laugh out loud. Why am I so good at embarrassing myself?

"Ha, I forgot how ticklish you are," Nia sputters as Tim and Shan break into a group chuckle.

Instead of turning bright red like usual, Nia's snorting laugh gets me going as well, and I relish the moment of pure happiness and absent worries. This is who I want to be: lighthearted, easygoing, and surrounded by people who are kind, not controlling. I spy Shan wiping a tear from his eye and take a moment to enjoy my stolen glance through the curtain of curls that have covered my eyes. Then I push them slightly, draping them to the side to hide my bruise while I attempt to tap into my confidence by daring to catch his eye.

In a mere moment, the sounds from the others fade away, and I am snatched into another world, somewhere only Shan and I exist, where the sadness of my past, and worry about what he thinks of my current state, disappear. These seconds drift by slowly. If rain had been falling, I'd be able to tap each droplet with the tip of my finger, allowing them to bounce into each other without busting as they descend toward the ground. It's like magic. Shan is there with me, his eyes locked with mine, the rise and fall of our chests matching, and I stay. I don't shy away. I don't run; I stay.

"April. Earth to April."

"It's no use. She's busy keeping Shan mesmerized." Tim's wheel squeaks as he moves back a tick and the spell is broken.

My darn hand, which isn't listening to what I want in the least, moves up and shifts my curls behind my ear. Shan's eyes move to the black and blue hidden poorly behind the beige gunk I have plastered on, and I downcast my eyes.

"Derrick's bad news. I hope you stay away from him for good this time. He doesn't deserve you, and no one deserves that." He nods his head at the alarming color beneath my skin.

Shan's words kindle a fire in my cheeks. I can't let him leave like this. What must he think of me? A girl who stayed with someone long enough to have to bring his mark with her wherever she goes. It will eventually fade, just as my feelings for Derrick finally dwindled and sputtered out, beaten away by his vicious words and cruel strikes.

"It's definitely over," I reply after a few seconds of silence. "Some people just can't change."

"Those are the ones who can do the most damage. It's the ones who love them that change."

We wave our goodbyes and offer up more "thank yous" to the guys. Nia and Tim exchange numbers for "study group purposes," she claims, and all I can think about as we leave that spot is the painstaking grief latched tightly around Shan's words. He's known someone just like me. Someone who has been hurt, maybe even worse than me. And here I am making eyes at him, when all I am doing is reminding him of her.

Chapter 3

Pushing It Away

The first mile is always the hardest. At least that's what I keep telling myself with lungs burning and a form that is totally out of whack. I trip more than once, running along the winding, dirt forest trail surrounding the university as I let my mind race.

My thoughts take a sprint through my body, blaming shoes that need replacing, or the warm-up I cut short, but I know the real reason. I took way too long to come to my senses with Derrick, and despite all of the group sessions, journaling, best-friend ice cream gorging cry-a-thons, I still beat myself up, or rather, I'm still allowing him, in some way, to hurt me.

My legs pound harder, erasing the salt drops before they can release from their fleshy, creased prisons, finding my stride once again, and catching glimpses of the rabbits (AKA the men's team) running up ahead. Sabrina and Caroline are usually with them as well, but their Greek activities have taken priority today. They've asked me to join, multiple times, but Derrick always talked me out of it.

"When will we have time to see each other with all of the sorority demands? Aren't we more important than some girls club? What about school?"

My ex wouldn't stop there. He'd bring up running and my love for art as well, using all of our private conversations against me in what eventually showed me that what it was really about was control. Control over me, over my time, and over what I shared with others about our relationship. He didn't want anyone to know, keeping his treatment of me, the slow, painful transmutation from being the doting, charming, hero to the jealous, cheating, anger-fueled beast of a boy-man. All this before I could see what was truly happening, before I could stop my fumbling fall over the cliff dropping down into a place where I've struggled to get out of for nearly a year.

My fingers ache as I picture myself clawing out of a relationship-grave meant to bury me alive, to trap me into a void where all I do sets him off, makes him react that way, causes him to push me, grab me, yelling until the spittle of his abusive mouth leaves my face soaked and tear-streaked.

"No one will ever believe you," he'd shout. "I've never left a mark on you."

That wasn't entirely true, but he knew how to hide them, where to land his attack, until now.

Lungs ignite, burning beautifully in the cool spring air. My legs join suit, not painfully, miraculously, and I power forward, gaining ground on the men's track team. Coach Gary typically sends Sabrina, Caroline, and I off with the guys more often now, pushing us to make our 4x800 the top in the state, and the nation. Not to mention the two-mile I painstakingly attack during the nearly eight round-and-rounds; the 3000 meters is like a beast trying to beat me down. Even more now that I relate my nearly inescapable relationship with Derrick to the heathen race. I travel the same road, over and over, where nothing ever changes and nothing ever will, but I keep trying, attempting to make it different. In a way, I desire to beat the track into submission.

Am I like Derrick? Abusing the track beneath my feet, crushing it down with each stride? The words Shan spoke are resonating more brutally honest than when they first hit my ears. Will I be forever changed now? Have I been shown that love is violence? I have been more aggressive lately on the track—vicious, even. Once even getting angry with Sabrina when she fell behind on the second leg. Though Caroline was upset as well. The three of us have to do our best since Mary struggles with the third leg, and I can't overcome deficiencies in two laps.

Ian's breathing propels me forward; I am nearly in line with him, will even pass him soon. The vicious April, creeping out of me, dragged forth by the chase. My mind and rest of my body catching fire along with my legs and lungs. This is dedication embodied in motion, my desire to win out of the gate. I surpass Ian, putting him behind me, along with the irritated growl he sends my way, while I keep my eyes on the back of Nate's blazing red hair. Passing him will get me closer to the main pack of the men's team, something I've always caught sight of but never joined, aside from warm-up. Yeah, that thing I basically skipped today.

"Hey, April," Nate pants, not turning his head to see who is coming alongside. He's the only one least annoyed by a girl passing him. Ian said nothing. "You going to hang out for a little or overachieve again today?"

"You know me. I'm allergic to slacking." My breathing is a silent wisp compared to Nate's inhales and exhales.

Nate's low-cut dreadlocks catch the strays of sunlight peeking through the leaves and needles of the forest trees. He's a kind guy. Having moved out here from Hawaii, he traded his surfboard in for a snowboard, at least during the school year. The sophomore returns every summer to rock the waves instead of the snow-covered rocks.

I like Nate; he treats me like a person and not a pair of breasts. Seems few other collegiate boys have this rare knack. His pace increases with mine, and we stay in sync for a bit before I move off ahead.

"Go get 'em, girl!"

An icy chill rolls through the trail, pushing against my face and pouring into my throat, settling down into my chest. For a split second, I bobble, just before finding my feet again and bolting toward the others. When the middle group stays together, they tend to forget the predator coming after them, safety in numbers giving them a false sense of security.

That's what Derrick has—safety in numbers, hidden by his soccer team, his coach, tutors, the legacies that endow the school with money from the lining of deep pockets that mimic those of his family. Note to self: being lavished with gifts from the get-go may be a sign of a way to get their claws into you for good. I should be clear about who I am referring to, though I am gathering it is clear by now. The ones who think they should be able to do with us whatever they want, whenever they want.

"Look at all these things I can buy you, take you to, provide for you, all in ways no one has ever done before," he'd say. "You are my Cinderella, and I am your prince."

Now, when I think of his words, I hear this instead. *We will be together always, even if you want to escape.*

Derrick has turned into the ultimate villain in my mind, the sinister equivalent of the anti-Disney male role. From one extreme to the other—one that doesn't exist, and one that unfortunately does.

My feet are floating now; I don't hit the ground—at least I don't seem to—but instead I fly, fly toward the others, gaining ground as their shoes become a serenade to my mind and body. It draws me in closer, demanding I join the chorus, become one with the team, leave my past and worries behind, find a means to create my own way, to break free of what has held me back. Shedding Derrick has done more for me than keeping him. He has not made me vicious; he has made me a fighter, a stronger, smarter, and happier warrior. I have learned my lesson, I have seen my errors along the way, and from here on out, I am powerful alone and will help any other woman who has faced the same as me, to be free—free to love, to hate, to be what nature intended. True to herself and never losing herself to a man.

Shan might be right, those left in the wake of abuse are changed forever, but that doesn't make me ruined; it makes me something new. Something I wasn't before, and I need to realize that's okay.

Chapter 4

A Chance Meeting

It's gotten easier, if that's even a good term to use. But "they" are right when "they" say time will help someone heal, from even some of the deepest wounds—at least for me it has.

It's been weeks since Derrick came after me with his little toy ball, and even though I can feel his eyes on me in class, burning and scathing, it doesn't have the same impact. More importantly, I have no inkling to forgive him or take him back this time, which means the time apart, this healing time, is for real this go-around. I'm not going back, and he isn't trying to change my mind.

On that subject, this does tend to cause me a bit of distress. A silent Derrick is a deadly Derrick. He's up to something; I just feel it. Even if he doesn't want me back, he certainly has too big of an ego to handle me not wanting *him* back. I'm a thing to him, and even though my confidence is blooming back into the daylight, soaking in the sun like a salve, I can't shake the itch in my mind that he's planning something.

That seed, digging away at the corners of my mind like a leech upon lake-soaked skin, is not going to distract me tonight. I've come too far, though it's honestly taking a good deal of my energy to keep myself from remembering the boy I thought I knew, to keep myself away from seeing those pictures in my mind of our first date, our first kiss, his touch (the nice ones, that is), the happier times before he changed. No, *changed* isn't the right word. Before he removed his perfect-boyfriend mask to show the monster beneath. It's harder than you think. I'm not a soldier. I haven't returned from a horrific war, but I have my battle scars, my own version of PTSD, and being alone now—or away from him, at least—should help. For some reason, though, the loneliness stays. Especially after not being on my own for so long. Others say I need this time. In the back of my mind, I know they're right, but my heart isn't always in agreement with those sentiments.

My fingers grip my sweater around my body tighter. I'd venture back to the table for something hot in this drafty room, but I can't seem to leave my seat. I almost chose not to come tonight after reading about the speaker who'll be joining us by video call. She's been in and out of the hospital since the accident that nearly took her life, instead taking that of her abuser merely a year ago. She had hoped to come in person, but circumstances have made it nearly impossible for her to leave home without distress. It's too horrifying to imagine someone who is supposed to love you doing something so terrible, but I know that could have been me, so I must hear her story. I must look into her eyes and show her she's not alone, and that we fight her fight.

I spy Janet at the coffee table, her delicate fingers trembling as she pours five ripped-open packs of sugar into her mug. Those of us who have made this support group a second family have a permanent home for their mug, the table in both a state of disarray and coziness reflected in their décor and small blemishes from repeated use.

I untangle my fingers from the holes they've created from the tight spaces between the soft, neutral yarn. I can't leave her up there like that. She's had it harder than most. She's older than me, in her early thirties, but a practically childlike marriage at the age of eighteen to her ex had him becoming more of her keeper than her husband. The years under his thumb stunted her in a way. She's learning how to do things without him, but it's a long road.

"Hi, Janet." My greeting is followed by a light touch on her arm, the one place she's finally able to stand without jumping. "If you put any more sugar in that tea, it's going to be hot liquid sugar."

Her fingers stop their motion toward the unopened sugar packets lined up in a white porcelain container. "It's going to be an emotional night. I debated coming tonight. It's still so new. I'm not even sure I should stay. My counselor said I'll know if I need to leave, but that I should take this time to try. I-I don't know."

"I'm nervous too, but I know this is going to be good for us, and for her."

"Yes, that's what Dr. Donna said."

"See, there you go. My psych class is paying off."

Janet snorts, tea nearly flying from her hands and her nose. "I only need one of those and I thought you were going pre-med?"

She means my parents want me to go pre-med. No, that's not fair; it's what I've always wanted as well. Every Halloween when I was little was spent in scrubs.

"I am. The major requires psych also, so I opted to take it in my elective slot this semester." What I really should say is that I was desperate to understand myself and to make sense of what Derrick was doing, but that would sound as dreadful from my lips as it does in my brain.

Janet whispers something I can't catch.

"I'm sorry, I didn't catch that." Do I want to know? Her furtive eyes tell me it must have something do with her ex-husband, Brian.

"I-I almost called him last night. I know, you don't have to say it, but I didn't do it and I wouldn't have. It's just…I had no one else for years, not that he was ever a good listener and basically told me everything was my fault, but I just, I just…"

I touch her lightly once more and then pull her a little closer. "I still listen to some of Derrick's old messages. The sweet ones. I don't know why, and I know it's not healthy, but I'll never judge you, Janet. Just, promise me you'll be careful. If you call him, he may be able to find out where you are."

The frail woman nods, her intricate braids creating a beautiful picture along with the pale pink dress that pops from her dark skin.

She's come a long way. Broken bones heal, but in her case, they healed awkwardly since he never allowed her to see a doctor. Some of her fingers are oddly angled and she has a bad back for a woman her age. They only had one car, and she could only ever use it if he was with her. She's a terrible driver because of it, but our group chipped in for lessons. It's the little wins that keep us going.

"I heard from my friend back home that he's found a new me. She's young, your age, barely in her twenties. I feel awful saying this, but I'm glad his attention has moved off of me," she admits while wringing her hands. "I'm awful. I mean that poor girl, but she knows about what he did to me and she doesn't care."

"That or he's convinced her that it's all lies. If he's anything like Derrick, that's their gift: lying."

"I sound like a total…bitch, don't I?"

"Why, Janet, such a potty mouth." My faux aghast includes a clutching hand to my chest topped off with prideful eyes. This woman wasn't allowed to even say *damn* in her own house. "And the answer is no. You don't sound like a bitch. You sound like a survivor. It's okay to be selfish, remember?"

"Doesn't it make things cockeyed for you sometimes? I mean care about yourself, and learn to say no, but also be empathetic, but not a pushover. Be assertive but not a…"

"A bitch?" We share a laugh and I steer my fellow survivor to our seats.

I know I'm one of the luckier ones in this group. A sliver of dread inches its way up my spine when I think about the woman we'll soon meet on the screen. It dances between my vertebrae, pushing and pulsing. I've felt this before, like a shock of intuition shaking me awake. She'll see us, we'll see her, but where most of our scars are hidden in our minds, hers will be out in front for all of us to see.

Janet's right, though. After you've been in an abusive relationship, you have to retrain your brain, and even then, we don't always react the way we hope or expect, but who can say they ever do? It's the frozen moment when someone does something awful, and you can't defend yourself, followed by the shame from

27

others when they can't see why you didn't do something—anything. Yell, scream, hit back, run...it's the shock. The deer being hurtled down upon by the wheeled monster's headlights. I'll never blame a person for what they did or didn't do in the moment of abuse or assault. Even those of us who think we are emboldened and strong can never guess how they might react. The girl inside of me who tears apart dirt and asphalt under her shoes didn't know what to do, and I'm sure my competitors would never picture me here. I sure as hell never did.

"Okay, everyone. We're about to begin. I'll allow Ms. Bends to introduce herself but please remember what we've talked about over the last few meetings," Mrs. Roberts—Kathy, she keeps telling me to call her—calls out. She never gave up on me. I owe her big time.

Kathy debated bringing in Ms. Bends, worried it would trigger us or trigger her. Regardless, she and the group ultimately decided we all need this.

"She can see us as much as we can see her," continues Kathy, her blond hair in perfect ringlets down her back. "She knows this is going to be emotional for you all and her, so tears are likely—hell, even sobs— but as we've worked on building ourselves up to not be ashamed of our scars, Ms. Bends' scars are wide open for everyone to see."

Pieces of ice shards travel down my back. The resulting shiver is impossible to hide, and Janet places her hand on mine where it rests on my knee and gives it a good squeeze. None of the stories we've heard in this room resulted in someone so scarred that they couldn't leave their home, let alone a death.

Kathy's eyes scan the room, no doubt gauging how everyone is doing as she prepares to bring this woman willing to bare her soul to all into our lives. "Can everyone see the screen well? Raise your hand if you can't, and we will help you get a better seat."

My eyes trace a path around the room to see the lack of hands in the air. It's eerily quiet, not the typical chatty beginnings of the group since everyone has become pretty comfortable with each other.

"Okay, well if we are all ready to go, I'm going to get her on the line and get started. Are there any last questions or concerns before we move forward?" The pause allows a crackle of energy to shoot throughout the air in the rec center basement. "Well, as we talked about last week, if you need to speak to someone or just need to take a break, Lena is in the back, and she's ready to help with anything you might need."

"This is it," whispers Janet, her hand pulling from mine to grasp her other one tightly enough to make it appear as if only fingers exist, as her nerves appear to take over.

"Can you hear and see us, Ms. Bends?"

My eyes leave Janet's hands and dart back to the screen. A woman with stark black hair and a pale face flickers onto the screen, like an older version of Snow White. She wears a brightly colored royal blue scarf on her head, which adds to the princess-like picture in my head. Something appears off about the shape of her nose, but it's her voice that nearly brings me to tears.

"I'm here, Kathy," Ms. Bends responds in a raspy voice while her hand moves slowly to her throat. "I apologize for my voice. I hope you all can hear me, and my best friend, Debbie, who happens to be a nurse is here to help if I need a break. Lucky her."

A laugh breaks out as Ms. Bends turns to look at someone off-screen.

"Well, it is wonderful to have you here with our group finally. Everyone has been eagerly awaiting this night, and I know I speak for each of us when I say thank you for taking the time to speak to us and for your bravery in being here."

Thank yous pour out, some in whispers, some in strong voices, others broken sounds from choked-back tears. Twinkly eyes look out from the TV screen to everyone in the room and land on mine.

I will not cry; I will not make this woman feel sad about herself after what her husband did to her. I won't.

Instead, I take a deep breath and smile. The slight quiver trembling my ribs on my inhale stays hidden by my bulky track sweatshirt. I catch Ms. Bends' eyes, or at least it seems like she's looking straight at me. Who can really tell in this sketchily lit room? But the tingle along my skin relays that she sees me as clearly as I see her and, at that moment, I know her. Is it that she's a reflection of where my life could have led? The familiarity lingers even as her eyes shift to others holding their breath in the room.

With the entrancement severed, I manage to break away from the screen to check on Janet. She appears still as stone, but I touch her hand, and she breathes.

"You okay?" I take her small nod and continued inhales and exhales as a good sign. We would have to be robots not to be impacted by the sight and sounds of Ms. Bends' brutal survival.

"Well then, we can get started," Kathy announces. "Ms. Bends, as you know, we are a group of survivors of abusive relationships. Some of us endured physical abuse, others mental, and most, I have found, have endured both. Many of us struggle every day, even years after a successful escape from the abuse. Can you share with us a little about your story and how you find the strength each day to move forward, to be so brave as you are today here with us?"

"Yes, of course. I'm pleased to be here today and to meet all of you. You have something special here in your group, and being here, committing to your safety and happiness is a huge step, and each of you should be very proud of yourselves. If I had been able to find something as you all have, I might have escaped the state you now find me in." The woman takes a deep breath, the inhale an obvious struggle. "Where to begin? Well, I guess the beginning is best. I met my ex-husband when I was sixteen, he was twenty, and I didn't listen to my parents or my older sister about our difference in age. Even my friends, for that matter. Soon they stopped trying to change my mind. That's what happens when you spend all of your time with one person and let your friends slip away. You lose your support system, unknowingly of course, because you're in love."

Head nods answer like a choir of angels singing the chorus to her song.

"I see I am not alone," she continues, with a smile not made of pity, rather, comprised of camaraderie. "My hope in being here today, something that would have been impossible for me a year ago, is twofold. For one, I wanted to prove to myself that my past can hold some good, that I can use it to help others such as yourselves. And the second is to help myself heal even further by getting the story out of my head and into the world instead of hiding as I did for years. Hiding caused more pain, as you can see."

With hands younger-looking than the shadow that falls on her face at times, she carefully reaches to remove her scarf. A collective intake of breath reverberates around the drafty room.

"It's kind of Frankenstein's monster-ish, isn't it?" Her fingers touch the area around the scar traversing her head, the hair growing around it making a jagged part at an odd angle. "I used to wear wigs, but those damn things are hot, and I don't want to hide any longer. These scars are part of me now, a reminder of what I have gone through, yes, but also a reminder of my survival."

I can't pull my eyes from the rough pale skin on her head. It begins in the middle and runs in an uneven pattern down before disappearing behind her ear. What in the world did he do to her?

"There's no easy way to say how all of this happened." Her delicate hands trace her head down to her throat. "The last time I saw my ex-husband alive was during another of his drunken nights when I was in the way. In the way of his grasping hands, in the way of the furniture. After crushing my windpipe and throwing me across the room into our glass table, he set the house on fire, with both of us inside. He hated himself, and he hated me for what he saw in my eyes while I lay there dying, so he sent us both into the flames. I survived, thanks to my son, but as for him, his remains were found—what was left of him anyway—and he is now finally in his version of peace. And so am I."

Warm rivers of tears form along both of my cheeks.

"I could have died."

I could have too.

"My son may not have stopped by that night."

He might not have stopped his knife that one time.

"But, I'm here. Here to tell you all that no matter how awful your past has been, you can start anew, you can be reborn, and even after years of surgeries, even though my voice will never be the same, and this stubborn scar refuses to grow hair anywhere near it, I am here. Even though my ankle was shattered and after six surgeries I am still wobbling when I try to balance, I am here. Where are you all?"

And without a thought, the answer echoes.

"We are here!"

"Yes, you are. And you are all beautiful, strong, amazing, talented, and forces of nature. Don't let anyone take that from you, ever. Stay the course, and you will never be in the situations you found yourself in before."

Applause and hoots flow freely between our crowd of twenty.

"I think I speak for all of us when I say, my God, you are a warrior, Ms. Bends," Kathy says.

"Please, call me Nicole, everyone. I didn't get here on my own, not by far. I have a group like yours up north, and thank goodness for them and their support. I'm also thankful beyond words for my oldest pulling me from the flames, and to Deb who has kicked my butt into rehab—like a drill sergeant, I might add—and wouldn't let me lie around feeling sorry for myself."

Nia is my drill sergeant. She's the one who found this group for me and encouraged me over and over again to go. I may be smart in some regards, but I was not using my head much at all. Thank goodness she was.

A dog barks off camera and Ms. Bends, Nicole, gives a tiny jump before waving the hand on her shoulder off gently. I know that feeling—the one of being on edge, even when you are at the absolute safest position you can be in, even when, for Nicole, the beast is dead.

"Mom?" The call coming through the speakers ignites something deep in my chest. It's as if my rib bones spread apart to handle the intake of breath rushing in. The odd reaction subsides, and Janet's hand moves away quickly from where it was touching my shoulder once I wave it away as Nicole did to Deb.

I see who must be Deb move behind Nicole, most likely to cut off the male voice seeking his mother. Yet Nicole's eyes light up in the opposite direction as a male frame comes into view—his arms hugging his mother tightly while his head drops to her shoulder. The head lifts from its resting spot and turns slowly, taking in the sight that must be his mother's computer and webcam, eyes widening at the realization that he's walked in on something he shouldn't have. The dark eyes dart around for a moment, unable to peel away from what he's just stumbled into before they connect with a pair of eyes that he knows.

Mine.

Chapter 5

Crack of Dawn

After waking up to the memory of Shan's eyes meeting mine for the hundredth time, I gave up on sleep. The sun will soon rise, and some of my team gets up for an extra early run on Sundays. It's like a sort of church service, and I need that about now.

The quickness at which Shan left the room yesterday was a blur, like the speed of light. He was there and then, nothing. Nothing but the look of pride and adoration on Nicole's face. On his mom's face.

"That was my son," she said with that radiant smile. "He saved my life that day. He doesn't like to talk about it much and I can see why. He may have saved me, but his dad also died that day. Even though they were at terrible odds, it is still a loss. I mourned as well."

Would I mourn Derrick if he died trying to kill me? I am sure there would be a period of sadness for the man I thought he was, and for Shan, the dad he wished he was.

I struggle with the coffee in the machine. I'm more of a tea person, so this contraption confuses the hell out of me. Thankfully, my roommate is pretty much never here, or she would kill me with all the noise I was making.

Shan. A hero. It doesn't surprise me. I can see him tearing into the burning house and carrying her out. How intense this all must be for him to handle. All of the pieces have fallen into place now. It must have been her on the phone most of the time. After the story she told, I'd answer every call from her as well. And with the numerous surgeries she's undergone, I am sure he's been on call all these years. All those times leaving chemistry lectures make even more sense; yet, with all of my daydreams about why he'd have to take the call, I would have never wished this upon him or his family.

The worst thing I am continually thinking about— the worst because it's so damn selfish of me—is that this is why he looked at me that day in lecture. When he caught sight of the bruise on my face, it must have come rushing back. Those times he saw his mom's own swellings of black and blue, or even saw his father strike his mom. Maybe even him. She didn't talk about Shan much after he left. It wasn't her story to tell. I'd be lying to myself if I said that I didn't dig deeper when I got back to my dorm. I flipped my laptop open faster than a beer bottle at a frat party and immersed myself in anything I could find on the case. How haunting it must be for the family after seeing similarities between Shan and his father, John Carp. Their height, build, hair, but I could also see plenty of Nicole. He may look like his dad, and still carry his last name, but from what I've witnessed and heard, that's where their similarities end.

After chugging down half a cup of straight black coffee, I wrestle with my uncomfortable sports bra, which is no different from every single one I own, and throw on my team jacket and shorts. My laces are a disaster—knots full off mud and dried leaves have me nearly cutting them off and relacing new ones. The knot finally gives and I shove my feet in, my eyes closing for

※

a moment to see the picture of Shan's face once again. A new knot forming, not in the laces, but in my heart.

I am going too fast, warp speed fast, and I know it. My lungs know it, and my legs for sure know it, but I don't care. The adrenaline from yesterday is helping me to keep up with the top pack.

Not only had Shan thrown me for a double flip, round-off, back handspring, his mother's words also find their way running laps around and around in my head. How the man she loved hurt her. How she knew he was dangerous, but she never thought he'd be capable of doing that. Did the courts care? No, John Carp was influential. Well known in their community, all rallied around him, thinking he could do no wrong. And do you think they came to Nicole's aid once the truth became disastrously revealed? No, instead they spoke more about what damage must have been done to him to trigger his madness. Meaning, what she had done to him. Taking Mr. Carp's children away. Leaving him before "till death do us part" became a new version of reality. Once the smoke and ashes cooled, Nicole changed her last name, moved her family away from that narrow-minded town, and made a new start elsewhere.

No one really speaks this early, which is perfect for me anyhow. The startled expression I can't shake must look like I've seen a zombie-ghost eating the brains of a vampire in a flaming pentagram. I've always been a little overdramatic. Thankfully the early hour makes everyone look similar, except for Sandy. Damn, that girl is always bright and chipper. I think she must have an espresso pump strapped to her central vein. She couldn't care less about why I hold a haunted look. Her eyes are for Ian. Too bad he's more in love with himself than he could ever be with anyone else. Almost makes me feel sorry for her, but I'm too busy wishing for just once that she would have a single bad hair day or a dark circle or two under her eyes.

I don't have to answer questions; that's the point of all of this rambling in my head. I mean what can I say? I would never tell Shan's secret. It isn't mine to share, and I don't want to ever share my secret—not to my team. I don't want to see their eyes looking at me in concern, or worse, pity or denial. Just as Shan's mom met skeptics and deniers of her own, I've had my share of nasty phone calls from Derrick's new conquest. Or had beer spilled on me "by mistake" when one of his soccer buddies passed by at one of the rare parties I've dared to attend since our final breakup nearly a month ago. They'd rather believe him than me, those guys who called me their friend.

Some people joke that they don't run unless they are being chased. Well, my past is haunting me, and the look on Shan's face mixed with the fearful story of his mother's near-death drive me to tear through this run at the ass-crack of dawn.

"Somewhere to be this morning?" Ian questions as I come up on his right. "You're not usually at our early morning jogs. Why change now? Something on your mind?"

"I don't know, Ian," I sneer. "It just sounded like a good idea when I woke up, pumped and ready to go at five a.m."

He stays on my flank, but I don't slow down to stay with him, his exertion apparent.

"I doubt that's it. Perhaps you can't sleep after being dumped by your soccer boyfriend. Heard you were the crazy jealous type. 'Psycho,' I think the guys were saying in the locker room."

If only I were graceful enough to somehow nail him right in the sack and keep running, I would have. Instead, I tense as I let the fearful April climb her way out again. The one who formed when Derrick got his claws wedged into the lobes of my brain. Worrying about what people were saying about me paralyzes my mind, which in turn slows my legs, leaving me with nothing to look at but Ian's back.

The chuckles from the swine in reflective running gear now ahead of me should have lit my fire, but the ungodly hour and lack of sleep slug into my muscles and take me down to an even lower gear.

Others pass me by, but it isn't until Sandy cheerfully catches up with me that I am able to comprehend the stupid pit of *poor me* I've fallen into this morning.

"Doesn't it feel wonderful out here? I mean, I didn't get to do my hair or anything, and I know I look dreadful without all my makeup, but it's worth it. Don't you think?"

I want to yell at her to keep her bright and cheery, Barbie-looking, *Sesame Street*-singing mouth shut, but that isn't going to help, and it's not who I am. She's only trying to be nice. Why does she like that creep Ian, anyhow?

Besides, she is right. Once I set aside the pictures of stupid jocks talking crap about me in the locker room and brought myself back to this moment, it was easier to feel the smooth, chilly air passing my face. It's crisp and warming with the slowly rising sun. Knowing Ian, he's saying anything and everything to get into my head, but I wouldn't put it past Derrick to shoot his mouth off in front of anyone who would listen. If it makes him look better, then why not?

I made a promise to myself, to my group, to Nia, and that promise was to eradicate the fearful April from my mind. A commitment to instead bring forward the courageous and brave April. The one who doesn't care what others think of her—especially college boys whose egos nearly always trump the truth.

"You're right, Sandy. It is an incredible morning. This six-a.m. stuff isn't so bad after all."

"Makes us stronger I say," she replies, looking at me slyly. "What do you say we gain back your ground. I feel like showing these boys a thing or two this morning, don't you?"

I'm starting to think Sandy isn't as clueless as her spunky, head-in-the-clouds portrayal makes her appear to be. We're all just playing a part at times, aren't we?

"Sounds like a plan. You know Ian's not good enough for you, right?"

"Yeah, I'm starting to see that. Cute guys need to realize their hotness wears off when they choose to be a dick."

I think I've misjudged Sandy.

Chapter 6

Unforeseen

I should have planned better before running off from my dorm without the necessities to catch a shower in the locker room where our run ends. Now that my adrenaline has worn off, and Sandy and I worked it to pass Ian just for fun, I'm done. The extra steps needed to get into hot water and clean clothes at my dorm across campus are easing the dread into my tired muscles and mucking up my mind. While everyone else is showering, I start my slow pace across the eerily quiet campus, the silence apparently another thing I didn't notice on my burst of sleep-deprived, over-caffeinated faux high.

The fog easing down from the mountains to wrap around our feet while we were running has swept away, leaving only the wet dew to kiss the sharp blades of grass. Feet echo behind me, sneakered feet, cautious versus determined feet. Not Derrick's feet. The fact that I know what it sounds like to be pursued by him curdles my stomach while easing my shoulders away from my ears. The steps stutter. Hesitating.

"Do you mind if I walk with you?"

Shan's voice sends smooth words, like warm, teasing wax throughout my mind before dripping down into my instantly tingly hidden spots. Thank goodness for this bulky sweatshirt and curse my surging hormones.

I realize I haven't turned around; instead, my feet choose to keep on going. Shan must think I'm ignoring him, so I will myself to stop moving, taking deep breaths to prepare to face him, to see his eyes, the eyes that widened when they saw me across the screen.

Managing to slow to the pace of a painted Vegas statue performer, I meet him with a shaky smile. "Hi, and um, yes, sure. I mean, I'd like that." Oh God, April, get it together!

"Join the early risers' run this morning? Don't think I've seen you join that one before."

Did his cheeks just flush?

"I mean I try to get here in the gym early on Sundays. It's dead in the weight room, so I usually see them leave. Not you, though. You don't usually leave with them, do you?"

His fumbling over words is easing my nerves. If I didn't know better, I would have thought he was doing it on purpose, but he's not Derrick. He's Shan. A nice guy. A hero.

"No, you're right, and I don't think you're a stalker for knowing, so don't worry." That's right, nice, light and flirty. *That was flirty, right? But didn't his dad stalk his mom? Crap! God, just stop overthinking and laugh. Ugh, not that type of laugh.* "I couldn't sleep and decided to drink coffee, which I never drink, so here I am."

Ta-da!

"Yeah, I couldn't sleep much either," he adds after a slight pause. "Look, no one really knows about my mom here, and I don't—"

"I'd never say anything," I jump in, touching his arm at the same time, just now realizing how close I am to him. "It's not my story to tell." We've never been this chummy, but it didn't feel wrong, so I didn't shy away, for once.

His eyes move from his arm to my face and back again. "Thanks. I figured you wouldn't. You don't seem like that type of person."

Now it's my turn to let blush hit my cheeks.

We walk for a while without saying a thing. The silence is pleasant. I don't feel the need to throw out words, and it also doesn't seem like anything is wrong just because we aren't talking. Birds become louder as the day warms, and we are able to spot a variety of them dashing around the campus trees and into nests in the eaves of the dorm. Everything seems right, in line with the comfort of our bodies walking side by side. His presence eases me to a state I've been unfamiliar with for quite some time now. It's a sense of protection, but without suffocation.

"Well, this is me." My words meaning two things, my home and me as a person, as we both look at the gray and brown stones of my building. "Do you still stay in campus athlete housing or did you move off campus?" I know this answer, but I don't want to seem like an actual stalker.

"I'm still on campus. It's the best deal for my family, and I'm closer to everything. I'm not normally much of a morning person. Sundays are different."

The weight of his comment makes my mind spin with gnat-like questions. When did Nicole say it happened? Was it a Sunday? Oh. Yes, it was. He looks up at the door to my dorm and back to my face. His smile lights up by the colorful rising of the sun against the smattering of feathered clouds. He's gorgeous, even more so when I can finally look into his eyes instead of stealing glances or knowing he was looking at me.

"How's your breakfast here?"

The same as every dorm is my first thought, but why would I say something so dumb when this may be him asking to come and join me inside. My mind jolts like a spark plug at the thought of having him joining me where I've only invited Derrick or my girlfriends.

It's just breakfast, April. Calm down. He wants to get to know you, and don't you want to know him better as well?

Of course, she does, you idiot. Don't you, April?

Oh great, now there's three of me. That's not going to go over well. I must look like I'm about to throw up, and I can see Shan's face shift from one of hopefulness to this-was-a-mistake.

Hurry, say something! says my first inner voice.

Just don't say anything stupid! Yep, that's the new girl. She's fun and super nice.

"It's great, I mean every cereal you could want, and I think they actually make real eggs on Sunday. Probably because not many of us make it down here early enough," I quip while miming the tilting back of the red Solo cup motion.

Stop that!

"Do you mind if I join you?"

"Yes, I mean no. No, I don't mind," I babble before taking a deep, stabilizing breath. "I'd love for you to join me."

I don't hold back on the loading of my tray with a full plate of eggs, bacon (kind of), and cereals of all types. The ladies helping the line, the ones who know me well enough to see the real importance of Shan next to me as we shuffle-step through the empty line, give me wide eyes when he looks away, and a few times when he doesn't. Mae had decided to overload my plate of eggs before moving on to Shan's, swiveling her head back and forth, resulting in fumbling of bouncy, yellow sponginess all over the counter.

If Shan notices, it doesn't show. He is a gentleman with each "thank you" and "have a wonderful day." I turn back as we walk away from the chattering ladies to see the many thumbs-up, and one ride-that-pony dance, which makes it tricky when I spin back around with a jiggling tray.

"They are much cooler here than in my dorm. I'm lucky to get a tablespoon of eggs at Letts Hall."

I freeze, and he freezes, the tension ratcheting up a notch between us.

"I'm sorry. I didn't mean to bring any of that into our time together."

Derrick's dorm is Letts Hall. It's townhomes for upperclassmen collegiate athletes or band members. How did I not know that they lived in the same place? Wait, why do I care?

Yeah, why do you care? He said "...our time together." Now enjoy it!

My lips shoot out a *pfft* and I wave my hand at the invisible memory of that tool, Derrick. "Don't worry about it. That's behind me now."

He smiles, but a mirrored crease around his eyes shows the doubt borne from his personal history with another woman who may have said the exact same words before a raging fire changed their lives forever.

I couldn't shy away from the look hidden behind that smile, holding my own as if the joy behind it could melt away any of the worries from his mind.

45

Don't ruin this, came the first voice.

Don't let him ruin this, came my new favorite voice.

"Told you they had real eggs. It's like a present and maybe another excuse for me to get my butt up for the Sunday runs."

My words tug a genuine smile loose from those incredible lips—a creaseless, worry-eye free smile that eases that tremor of tension in the air from the ghost of Derrick past.

"This is a hundred times better than my usual Sunday."

Cue my goofy, overly excited grin. "It's a date."

You go, girl!

Chapter 7

Date Night

So, this is a date—a true and real date with a guy who isn't only thinking of himself, who isn't trying to control me and everything and everyone else.

This is our first real date where it's just the two of us. Over the last month, we've had three Sundays in a row at breakfast and meeting out with friends, on top of the constant texting or phone calls every day. Tonight is different. I've had him all to myself; first for a movie, and now we are enjoying each other—oh, and our dinner. Thank God he likes movies. Derrick would go, but he was obnoxious the whole time and had no interest in the ones I wanted to see. He instead treated it like we were in a hotel room, groping me even with people on both sides of us. When I'd put a stop to it, he'd be pissed and start a fight with me about how I don't really love him before dropping me off at home and giving me the silent treatment for days. Warning signs. Lots of warning signs. And all the while he was hooking up with other girls on the side, probably excusing them by thinking I needed to be put in my place for not fanning his ego enough.

But with Shan, it is so much easier. Before tonight, he asked me what I wanted to see, and we easily agreed on a fantasy adventure flick. Afterward, we found our way to this cute, quiet pho restaurant—another thing the "other" guy would never want to do. His interest in culinary adventures was limited, and if Derrick didn't want to, it didn't happen. More warning signs.

The moments of Shan's worried eyes creeping into our time together started to fade away slowly over the course of the evening. He even spoke about his mom more before our soup came, which made asking more questions about his life even easier.

"Do you have any siblings?" I ask while trying to delicately wrangle a bean sprout and noodle at the same time.

"I have a younger sister—she's still in high school at a private school out of the country. I'm sure she'll be home for her senior year."

I don't pry into the reasons why she's away, and I try not to assume.

"She's a badass," he says proudly. "You should see one of her basketball games. She's better than I ever was, better than most of the guys on my team when I played in high school."

"I'd love to go. It's a winter sport, right?" Yes, please tell me we will still be having this much fun come winter.

"Yeah, we can do some skiing or sledding when you come," Shan suggests, snacking on a bean sprout. "It's sick up there in the winter. We get great snow."

"I haven't skied in forever, but I did enjoy snowboarding in high school. Might have been on my butt quite a bit." I laugh, the chopsticks in my hand making various circles in my bowl. "But I'd do it again."

"Great!" he exclaims before raising his glass to cheers with mine. "I bet you are adorable in snow gear. You look good in everything."

Now I'm blushing.

"I have to admit," Shan adds, perhaps noticing that I am too stunned to speak, "I haven't been able to stop staring at you tonight. I hope that hasn't been too obvious or creepy. It was hard not to do the same thing when you weren't available, but I managed when I could. Even took a lacrosse ball in the arm a couple of times, watching you run. But I have to admit, getting to know you, and not just wishing I did, has made you even more beautiful to me."

"I—I feel the same way," I stutter before taking a deep, settling breath. "Any time you passed me in class or when I saw you at lacrosse practice, I couldn't help but watch you. I've been drawn to you, and it's even stronger now."

Shan's eyes light up at my admissions. "I only want to be with you, April, and I hope you feel the same way. And if you are ever worried about trusting me or thinking I would ever do anything like that jackass Derrick, I promise I will never hurt you," he says with a finger tap on the table. "You know that my mom went through something terrible, and I don't want you to ever feel anything close to that ever again, and I will never let anything happen to you."

Gulp

"I knew before we met that you were kind and just a good guy. Word gets around, and I'm glad no one snatched you up before I got my head on straight." How I wish I would have gotten it on right sooner. "Knowing what I do now about your family, I can't express how sorry I am. If I can ever help, in any way, please let me know. Don't ever feel like you can't talk about it with me just because of my past. I want to be here for you as much as you have promised to be for me."

A sexy smile passes over Shan's lips. Derrick would have never expressed himself like this to me, and it makes the man across from me even more tempting. Shan reaches his hands across the table to take mine. I shiver when his thumb passes over my knuckles.

"I'm glad it's just you and me tonight," he says, interlacing our fingers. "It's been nice hanging out with our friends, and you have some great ones. Nia's funny and I can tell she has your back, but I admit I am enjoying this time alone to really get to know you."

"Me too," I reply while moving my fingers against his. I don't ever want to let go. "Nia likes you, and so do I."

"I like you too. I've never felt like this before. You're really amazing, April. I hope you know that."

The waiter ambles over to us, fidgeting and looking around the room before flicking the long bangs of his black hair from his eyes. "Do you have the green Jeep in the parking lot?"

And there goes my stomach, straight down to my knees.

"Yes. Did I leave my lights on or something?" Shan is already preparing to rise to his feet before looking out the windows. His jaw muscles are pulsing tightly, like a mesmerizing blinking light. He senses, as well as I do, that it isn't his lights. The ghost of Derrick, popping up in corporeal form this time, begins to rear its ugly head.

Grabbing my hand and keeping me close, he leads me to the door. His presence brings my tremors down a tad, and it isn't dominating, nor does it make me feel weak. We are more of a united front as we push open

50

the door, both of us sweeping our gazes in all directions just in case. Prepared as I thought I was for what I'd see, my visions weren't even close to what has happened to Shan's car. Orange and yellow paint has been poured, tossed, splattered all over the dark green tint of the older SUV. The colors blend together and look like flowing of lava, with the dark paint of the car resembling charred earth.

"Oh God, Shan, I am so sorry. This is all my fault." It had to be Derrick. He has been silent for weeks, but I got a text from an unknown number yesterday and all it said was *slut*. He knew about Shan and me, and even though he had been seeing plenty of other girls while, and since, we dated, he is still trying to control my life.

"This isn't your fault. We don't even know who did it. It could just be a prank from CU. These are their colors, and we play them again soon. They're just trying to get into my head."

My eyes meet his, and he gives me a half smile, one that is mirrored in the wistfulness of my own, both of us wishing we could live a life together without the baggage of the past.

"Even if it was him, I'm sure they have cameras, and we can get this sorted out. Plus"—he smiles wider this time—"I've got insurance. Mom keeps bugging me about using my, I mean, the other car…" Darkness flickers across his face. "Just can't manage to get inside of it again."

My fingers touch his arm, his shoulder, and then his face. He turns to me, bending down to lessen the four inches of space between us. As if the paint, a dripping sunset, is on fire, its flame licks along my cheeks, down my neck, before traveling down to my stomach. When our lips open in tandem and touch, I release a primitive

51

moan before we deepen the kiss. With tips of tongues touching and hands gripping each other tighter, we become lost in our first kiss. If Derrick plans to drive us apart, Shan's reaction foils that plan.

A nagging worry attempts to interrupt our moment, telling me this may be a goodbye kiss, one hell of one, but one nonetheless. I push back that doomsday nagger and press myself against him even more than before.

Now it's his turn to moan. Goodbye kiss, meet *hello* kiss.

"Uber?"

"Uber," I agree.

"I can call the insurance guy in the car, but I need to snap a few pictures first. Then, to my house?"

I nod and dislodge myself from his embrace before clicking open the app to order the car.

My eyes spy a new text message notification, and dread delivers bile up my throat and into my mouth. Tapping the message app slowly, I am relieved to see the note from Nia. A quick confirmation back to her that we can study tomorrow night is followed by a berating chuckle for being so on edge. Shan is probably right; the rivalry between our schools isn't unheard of, and he's one of the starters kicking ass this year for our team. Cheap shot, yes. Guess we'll have to see what the cameras show.

I walk around the front of the building, looking at the cameras, when our waiter comes out to check on things, too.

"Boss says there's no footage and sent me out here to look."

I gaze at the small lens of the camera closer and realize the reflection of it is minimal, not one that the glass camera eye should beam back from the lights shining in the darkness. This one has been painted black. These guys have thought of everything. I bet they had masks on as well.

The employee moves off to tell Shan the not-so-good news, so my mind travels, allowing a visual story to unfold. Maybe it's a fantasy just to cover up that gnawing feeling that Derrick is behind everything, but who cares. The vision of college kids in yellow masks, spray paint, and a rivalry target brings me peace. Delusional peace, maybe, but peace, damn it.

Shan snaps about a hundred pics and begins uploading them to his insurance app. A tow truck will take the car, and we will hop in an Uber to his townhome. Yes, one of his roommates would be there, but he'd be meeting his girl soon. We'll have privacy, and time—lots of time.

This all sounds thrilling, but also frightening. Aside from some hand-holding and that kiss, we've been extremely PG—hell, G even. Even those dang princess kisses! I have enjoyed our slowly building momentum to this night, a night when something so wrong is transforming into the next step in our relationship. I don't know what it means, and where it will go, but I am ready. I've even started wearing underwear that doesn't look athletic or made for comfort and comfort alone—satin and lace, and even with a matching bra. Don't get me wrong; I like the way I feel in them just as much as the thought of what Shan will be thinking seeing them, which is the way it's supposed to be, right? Just part of making sure I'm the person I was BD (that's before Derrick): feminine and confident. The way Derrick used to touch me and treat me was totally opposite once he shed his snakeskin and showed his true self. Then began the rabid jealousy if I dressed in a way he thought was meant to draw attention to myself.

"Who were you talking to dressed like that? Are you trying to make him think about getting in your pants? I saw you talking to him and smiling. You looked like a slut asking for it."

Not only did his words lead me to morph into a someone who faded into the background, but I also began to realize I was doing it to peel Derrick's eyes and fingers off me as well—his idea of lovemaking turned toxic.

"Well, that was easy."

I breathe easier once Shan breaks into my nightmare reverie. Where did the destructive idiots in masks go? Damn mind, damn Derrick. When will his talons dislodge from my brain?

Maybe after tonight, bow chicka bow wow.

"Stop that." I laugh to no one before I turn around to eye the guy I am literally going home with tonight.

All night?

"Did you say something?"

"What, oh yeah, nothing. Just mumbling to myself."

"Telling yourself anything interesting?"

Gulp. "No—well yes."

Now he's looking at me, confused. Concerned maybe. "The insurance app made it super easy to get everything rolling. How's the car coming? I'm sure we have a wait, since it's the weekend."

"Five minutes out."

He responds with a smile that melts the insides of my thighs into worse than jelly—more like hot wax.

Heading back to the Letts Hall athletic housing in the car is at times quiet, but not an uncomfortable

54

silence—more like a buildup of excitement and need for what's to come. I don't have many partners in my past, and the memory of Derrick is something I'm hoping time with Shan will erase for good.

As we pull up to Shan's townhome, lights glow through his windows, triggering the jumping of my nerves from my stomach to my throat and back again like I'm on a sick, nausea-inducing, internal trampoline. I know his roommates; we've all hung out before. I don't get why any of that would bother me, though the way Derrick spoke to me in front of his friends and how they, in turn, treated me at times still makes me nervous. When will I stop living my relationship with Derrick on an endless loop as I move forward with Shan?

He senses my unease, as if it's easy to detect the sticky thronging weight of it hanging around me, not to mention I'm certain that he can hear the stomach noises bubbling up and gurgling in the body next to him in the small sedan. Not hearing a thing or deciding gallantly not to care, he grabs my hand, kissing the top of each knuckle as they slowly bump toward his lips.

"I can take you home if you want." His face is sincere, though I can tell by the playful smile partially hidden by the straight line of his lips that he's hoping I haven't changed my mind.

"No, I want to come inside."

The open door sends smells of pizza, no, Ray's calzones, beer, and college-guy scents wafting into my nostrils. Odors are rude that way.

"Hey, Shan! April!" his roommate Tyler hollers from the couch.

Tyler is by far one of my favorites of Shan's friends. He doesn't play lacrosse anymore, but Shan and the others would never want to boot him out. It may be because he's an amazing student and why get rid of that type of study buddy? The coach made him a team tutor or something, so he gets to stay.

Tyler gives me a bear hug, expertly managing not to spill his cup halfway down my back or on his long hair or overly bushy, and still growing, beard.

"Looks like this is becoming its own entity, Tyler." I give the beard a gentle tug, and his eyes twinkle. Derrick would make me pay if I did that in front of him or if he ever heard about it from one of his goons. Shan just laughs.

"Yeah, we think it's eating some of the food," Shan adds. "Though that may be Dre-Money. The kid can eat!"

"Shan's not kidding, girl." Tyler snickers. "Watch your food when you're here with Dre. He's out right now, doin' what playas do."

We all laugh and sit around the living room on mismatched couches and folding chairs that really pop against the zebra print rug under the glass table. Conversation is easy while we snack on salsa and chips and a bowl of what looks like some sort of trail mix bar snack.

"See, Dre snagged those from The Station. Even his favorite bar is his snack machine."

"So, where's Michele? I thought you guys had gotten back together." I give Tyler a playful smack on his arm, and he answers with a knowing smile.

I served as a sort of relationship counselor between the two, helping them work through some of their drama. By drama I mean some of Michele's tendencies to be an overactive flirt and Tyler's green eyes, face, bulging-bicep jealousy that would overwhelm him more

56

than he wanted. They both gave in a little. Knowing that Michele's actions were innocent, Tyler was able to accept her the way she was. It's one of the reasons he's my favorite so far. A man that can let a woman be herself is the best type of man.

"She should be ready for me to head out to meet her soon. She's out with the girls and look at me—I haven't even texted her more than twice tonight." He shows me his phone with two unanswered texts from Michele, his face only twitching a tiny bit at the strain his fingers must be under as they manage to refrain from texting her again.

He loves her, she's his everything, and she loves him. As he learns to trust her even more, they grow into a stronger couple each day. Who would have thought I'd be helping someone with their relationship? Maybe it's because they both know a little about my background with Derrick. It allows them to grasp and respect my opinion and guidance, even if comes from someone who's been in the trenches. The last thing Tyler would ever want to do is hurt Michele. The studious heartthrob was thinking more about rearranging the face of the boy getting her attention and wanting to act on it.

People can change; Tyler's a perfect example of wanting to for love and for the good of a relationship with someone he respects. Helping the couple has been good for Shan and me as well. I think it proves to him that I've grown away from the time I lost myself with Derrick. Yes, the memories still hurt and make me fearful of closeness with someone new, especially with intimacy, which is staring me straight in the kisser tonight, but I won't go back to him—never again. Not much time may have passed since we were together, but

I'm already a new person, no longer the shell I once was in Derrick's presence.

"I'd like to show you something." Shan stands and reaches his hand out for me to grasp with my tiny hand in comparison.

Tyler's beer bubbles dare to come out his nose and instead make him choke a little as he quickly exits the room at Shan's request.

"Grow up, Tyler," Shan calls over his shoulder.

The man of my dreams pulls me along gently, and I move without a second thought; well, the thought was there but my number two stepped on her throat before she could act like a wild horse bucking around wildly at the thought of being corralled as if it were the same as the mere idea of being in a boy's room. Not a boy, a man. My man, I guess.

Shan is the guy I've been sneaking eyes at for a couple of years now, and after a few light touches and one spectacular kiss, I know I'm ready for something more. I'm not sure how much more, but the pictures in my head of pressing my skin against his in areas we never have before shoot a spastic thrill along my skin while a sizzling, metal sparkler sizzles to life in my mind.

Chapter 8

What I've Been Missing

We walk through the maze of his house. The three-level townhome is difficult to navigate, with tight stairways and corners, but we manage with held hands. The anticipation bubbling in my lungs causes my breathing to vary from slow panting trills to speedy silent gasps of air.

Breathe, dammit. Don't pass out and embarrass us.

He stops in front of a badly stained wood door covered in stickers and what looks like splatters of paint. Aside from my friends since grade school, I've only been in a guy's room twice, for this type of reason. Of course, there are parties in dorm rooms and study sessions, but we aren't here for either of those intentions.

Thankfully. Nerd.

When he opens the door, I smile at a tidy desk, which takes up a small wall, and the disarray of his bed and closet on the opposite side.

"Ah, let me take care of this real quick. Stereo is over there if you want to put something on."

"I thought a person's stereo was sacred."

"Yeah," he responds playfully. "This is a big step for me."

"Well, I'm flattered."

My finger plays along the screen to open his library of music. Flashes of touching Shan's skin with the same fingertips flicker into my mind's eye, and I shiver.

"Are you cold?"

I keep my back to him, only shaking my head as I shyly smile at the physical reaction that just the thought of him teases from every part of my body.

I turn on an Avicii song and move toward the man making his bed and tossing the small clutter of clothes into his closet before shoving the door closed with his sneakered foot.

"I love this one."

"Yes," I agree. "Gone too soon, that's for sure." What was I thinking putting on a song from a guy who took his life? That's exactly what his dad did, and then here I am pointing it out with a giant billboard. When will I get this tact thing down?

Sometimes you don't need words to be tactful.

Following inner voice two's orders, I walk toward Shan, his hands full of the remaining socks, and a random shoe falls from his hands when he sees the intent on my face.

I reach out to touch his chest, and this time it's his turn to shiver. My hand runs up his neck, along the curve and around his back as he lifts me onto my toes. The kiss is light, but gradually transforms into something close—nope, beyond what I was enjoying in the parking lot. His arms, wrapped around my waist, give a pleasant pressure, allowing the length of my body to press against his to create a fiery explosion of need in the dark, warm places of my body and soul.

See, I can handle this, no problemo.

I lean into him at first, moving us toward his bed and then pulling away from our dancing lips to see the sexy smirk on his face and the sparkle in his dark eyes. One arm releases my waist, but the other grips me enough to hold my weight as we lower down onto the bed, his free hand keeping us from flopping upon the down comforter as I straddle him on the edge.

Kissing me again, Shan runs his hand through my hair. He plays with the curls through his fingers, and I grimace when the knots keep them from smoothly flowing through to the ends.

"I love your hair."

"Thank you."

"And I love these." His comment brings his mouth to mine again. Shan's lips don't overwhelm mine; instead, they move against each other in a perfect formation. Even the flick of his tongue finding mine manages to be passionate, not aggressive. Kissing Derrick in this way was more about possession, and I smile into his kiss at my happiness in knowing and experiencing the difference.

"How'd I get so lucky?" My question slips into the moment as we both break for air to get the chance to look into each other's eyes. His gaze is mesmerizing.

"I think you have that backwards."

The motion of my hips moving toward his takes us down completely, each triggered part of my body aching as they slowly touch his answering need. I rub against him and his hands find my backside, pushing me into him as our kisses continue. When his mouth breaks from mine, he finds my neck, and I arch backwards to allow him access to my collarbone and shoulder. He rolls onto his side. The movement, which flusters me at first with his absence, leads to his fingertips following his kisses down my shoulder and then traveling all the way down my arm before finding my hip and then the hem of my shirt.

"Is this okay?" he asks when our eyes meet.

Tell him it's okay!

"Yes, more than okay."

The tickling tips of each finger bring first the chill and then the heat as they make their way along the sides of my stomach before their *tap dip tap dip* along each of my ribs. My body writhes against him as his fingers graze the bottom of my bra.

Shan's hand moves up, touching the soft fabric, truly a barely there barrier between my flesh and his. My nipples respond to his touch, peaking and throbbing toward each motion of his fingertips. Sometimes he squeezes and pinches a little and other times just softly rubs, making my body react and continue to squirm. I lift my leg to go over his hip, moving me even closer to a growing need inside the both of us. Unable to contain the restriction of my shirt, I pull away slowly and lift it up over my head.

I shrug at him and he smiles, pulling me back closer to him before breaking away with a shake of his head and removing his shirt too. I take a second with my hand placed on him to explore his chest and stomach with my eyes. I've been around athletes most of my life, but nothing compares to the shapes, curves, and bulges in all the right places along his shoulders, arms, chest, and abs. I blush at the ideas I have tumbling into my awareness like mini picture shows. The images prompt me to roll toward him, close enough to kiss his bare chest. A relaxed groan escapes his lips as I move my way up to his neck, finding a place to clamp my teeth against on one of his lower ear lobes.

His skin smells and tastes unreal and thankfully not bathed in cologne or aftershave. No, it's only him. His pure, manly smell that will forever remind me of this moment, of the texture of his skin against mine, his breath hitting me, and along with all the passion is an underlying safety.

His moans change into a humored annoyance at the fact that he can't reach me as I spend time gracing his body with kisses and roaming my hands on every inch of his upper body. Knowing I'm arousing him and feeling the pressure of his fingertips digging into my hip, I back away with a sneaky smile, and he devours my lips before tumbling on top of me while continuing our soft yet impassioned kiss.

This man, this incredibly sexy man, grinds against me gently, yet firm enough I can feel his growing want within his jeans even more so. Visions in my mind tempt a yearning to see him fully.

His lustfully lidded eyes swivel from direct contact with my own to sliding away to fixate on a puzzle he longs to solve—the silver clasp in front of my bra.

"May I?" he asks with a questioning eyebrow lifting on one side of his face.

I nod in agreement, both nervous and excited about the desires readying to unleash once my undergarment disappears.

Soft, firm fingers trail along my stomach, moving slowly between my rib cage and the clasp. And then, a soft *click*, the faint sound translating into a freedom bell within my overly stimulated being.

I can't remember the last time I was touched so gently and passionately. Perhaps I have been before now, but everything seems deleted after the pain that came after. And the boys I kissed in high school seem a lifetime away, ages ago and innocent. Nothing like the unfolding sensuality of this night.

Shan's fingers slide down the straps between him and my expectant breasts. It isn't cold in the room, far from it, yet my nipples ache as if I've just walked outside in a twenty-degree day, topped with windchill. It's taking an immense amount of focus to stay still as he looks over my half-naked body, but I can feel the little trembles, small waves gaining magnitude as if on the brink of a full-on earthquake. The heat his sultry gaze manages to invoke in me makes me squirm more than the idea of being completely exposed on top.

"You are beautiful, April," Shan whispers as his eyes travel between staring into mine and slowly looking down my neck all the way down the rise and fall of my bare chest.

The words take all thought from my mind; I'm suddenly blank. Completely dumbed down to my basic needs of love, sex, and, well what else is there again? The primordial state of my attention flickers back and forth amid the undeniable force of his lustful gaze and the tenderness of his fingers—or are they feathers—gliding along each section of my body, scarcely staying long enough in one spot.

"So are you." These fumbling words earn me a ravenous, deep kiss on my lips, before his mouth travels down my chin, my neck, and on to the depression in my collarbone before heating the skin in the valley between my breasts.

While his lips move down, one of his hands caresses up my side before hungrily grasping onto my left breast. It's been too long since I've yearned to be with someone like this; well, wait, I've never been with someone like this.

With one hand busily caressing one side of my chest, Shan brings his lips to the outside of my breast, creating a circle of desire in his wake while his path spins inward until he makes his way to the core of my breast. Flicking and licking my nipple with ease, he changes course and the graze of his teeth shoots a line of liquid heat down my body. I gasp, arching my back and digging the heels of my feet into the cover, raking the soft, thick blanket into a mess that hides carnal secrets in each wrinkle.

"Mmm..." I manage between my first jaw-snapping cry and before my lips find themselves bitten between my teeth.

"Is this okay? I mean it seems like this is more than okay, but I'm just checking." He chuckles and I take my arms that have been spread sloppily behind my head, to loop around the back of his neck with a desire-laced squeeze.

"I just hope I'm not squirming too much," I manage.

"I don't think such a thing could exist. It feels so good to know that your body is enjoying this. I know I am. I'm certain I can make it feel even better if you want."

I nod in agreement before he dives deliciously onto my breasts once again. My head spins as his lips perform hopscotching kisses from one side to the other while his thumb dips into the moistness and teases. Shan pulls on my right nipple with his teeth, sucking and pulling me into a crazed state. No words form, only groans and teeth-grinds to the backdrop of the shifting noises from the comforter moving beneath my squirming body.

I rotate my hips in circles, pushing upward and down and all around, enjoying the feel of his hardness pressing against me.

Shan rolls a little to the side, leaving me colder than when his body lay atop me and even more so as his fingers play between my breasts, squeezing and pulling and appreciating them enthusiastically. From there he starts to walk two fingers down my stomach, moving back and forth between my hips. Shan turns to me suddenly, the movement prying both of our eyes from his fingers. He looks into my eyes before going down once again to ravage my breasts with his mouth. While his lips keep busy, those hands of his find the waistband of my jeans while individual fingers play underneath, peeking in and back out again, and I can't keep the thoughts about the fingers playing somewhere else. I move one of my hands on top of his and shift it slightly deeper into the waistband of my pants. His kisses break away from my chest and his gaze meets mine with a kid-in-a-candy-shop smile.

"Are you sure?"

"Extremely."

His hand plunges deeper underneath the top of my pants before yanking back out to unfasten my jeans. Now, revealing the lacy panties I have that match the bra, his hand plays along the outside of the lace-covered satin. The fabric stays pressed against me by the wetness he's slowly eliciting from my body. When his fingertips press into the richest part of my sex, it's as if the dainty fabric disappears and the impact of the action forces a growl to escape his lips.

And in that split second, passion takes over when he moves his hands from the top of my underwear, instead diving underneath to find the wetness that has been building inside me all along. His mouth finds mine once again while his hands inch down between my legs. The excitement of what's to come builds the intensity of our kiss with lips, tongue, and sometimes a nibble from teeth, a pleasant surprise when it comes from me. Shan grazes his fingers around the outside of the center of my wet heat before finally dipping his fingers deep inside.

My back arches and, for the life of me, I can't deny that everything leading up to this moment has me close to a climax right then and there. I pull from our kiss at the dizzying effect the pressure of both pleasure and pain are creating inside of every cell in my body. With my head to the side, I begin to pant as I push and pull against his fingers, moving against them in time with his pulses. It's like a dance. Push and pull, push and pull, and I can't hold back the firing signals in both my body and mind that want to come so soon.

It's been so long, and never like this.

No. Never.

"Go ahead, sweetheart. I want to feel you. Please. For me."

My God, even his words are bringing me to the brink. How is this possible? I don't even remember climaxing like this before. There's something raw and nearly mystical about it all. As if some destiny that kept Shan and I apart has finally been fulfilled, and I am overflowing with desire and need.

I don't hold back any longer and succumb to the pulsing flow of ecstasy. I cry out, muffled by my draping arm, that has once again managed to just flop around wherever. Shan's fingers leave the overflowing heat from deep inside of me and he pulls me over until I am lying down on top of him. With his fingers moving through my hair, he smiles—a drop-dead-gorgeous, you-are-amazing smile—before focusing on pressing his blazing lips against mine. I shudder beneath his warm body, unable to contain the intensity in the increased seismic waves that have been unleashed by his touch.

"You are amazing," he murmurs once there's a short break between our kisses. "I've already adored so many things about you, and now, being with you like this makes me truly believe you and I work, don't you?"

Um, hell yeah we do!

"In more ways than I can count. If you can count right now, but thinking is a bit hard."

We both laugh and I let my head fall behind his shoulder, our bodies pressed together like two perfect puzzle pieces, two hearts broken by a past that mold back together as one. I can't say it yet—it's so soon— but I think I love this man. I think I can love him forever if he lets me, if our lives and the world around us lets us. I squeeze into him, taking in his warmth and the safety like no other in his arms.

"You don't have to go, you know. You could stay here tonight."

I move my hands to push up to hover above the body of the man I couldn't even speak to just a couple of months ago, and now, here I am, in his bed and being asked to stay with him, all the while knowing there's nothing else in the world I'd like more.

"There's nowhere else I'd rather be."

Chapter 9

A New Point of View

I hadn't slept that soundly in months. Every bump outside my dorm room or late-night text from a drunk friend set me on edge. But not last night. Last night I was snuggled against a man who hasn't given me a second thought or concern about his intentions or the type of person he is on the surface, and deep down where light hasn't completely shown me everything. That part doesn't bother me, because I know the warning signs now, and Shan hasn't flared one to life in the least.

"I don't want to get up." His muffled voice moves my hair and tumbles against my back in our spooning position.

"I don't want to leave."

"Damn having commitments. They're overrated."

"Totally overrated." I chuckle while turning to see his sleepy morning face. Can he get any sexier?

I'm sure he can. And there's the instant blush.

"You can't miss your game, though, and I have to get my other work done before studying with Nia since our make-up meet is tomorrow."

"Would they even notice if we weren't there? We could just lock ourselves in here and order delivery. I've got tons of movies. We never have to leave the bed."

"Very tempting, sir. I will take you up on this offer when it's not at your expense or at the risk of Coach Stevens coming after me." I grit my teeth. "I've heard the stories. Didn't he make you guys promise to be celibate once?"

"That's just a rumor. I think he started it to scare everyone into keeping their wits about them during the season."

"Well, it's not working so well on somebody, now is it? And what if it's true?" My mock gasp sells the horror along with a clutch of fingers to my chest. Shan, on the other hand, looks like he's about to burst. I may have over-tipped my hand.

His hands push against my back end and our mouths meet in heated desire.

"I'm not going to risk it." Cue melting things I can't explain and throbbing things to clench in my depths.

"I'd hope not."

A growl this time and I'm instantly on top of him, donned only in one of his shirts and my underwear.

He holds my face in his hands, pulling himself up to meet my lips and to whisper into my ear. "I can't wait to be with you again."

"Me either."

After using my finger to brush my teeth and lots of mouthwash, I crawl back into my clothes and lace up my shoes. Something stirs inside; a dread as a nagging pain, more like a headache that never fully goes away, creeps around like a thief in my brain.

Shan walks over to me where I sit at his desk chair and spins me so I'm facing him. He stands shirtless in front of me, holding his jersey in his hand.

"I'm sorry I can't make your game today. Next week, I promise."

70

My attempt at distracting myself from my own thoughts doesn't work on his quick mind, though looking him up and down is distracting. "Though, if you are playing shirts and skins, I may have to blow off anything that might have mattered five seconds ago."

His chuckle is heart-melting.

"What's really on your mind? I can tell when you're lost in there, you know. We've been around each other long enough now for me to pick up on these kinds of things, plus, it's kind of second nature."

Though his face is sweet, plastered with a questioning concern, I cringe. How long will he want to put up with the shade of Derrick in our lives? He says it's second nature to him because he saw this same look of fear in his mother's eyes one too many times. He doesn't talk about it much, still, so I don't know if he's holding back for me or for him.

"I'm just a little concerned, especially since we don't know for sure who wrecked your car, that if I'm seen leaving here it'll just unleash more drama." My head drops to the hands holding each other above my lap. "It's not fair that you have to deal with my baggage."

Taking my hands in his strong ones, he brings me up to standing. My chest blossoms when I look up at him.

"Don't ever feel like you need to be ashamed about your past." His voice is soft, along with the fingertip that raises my downcast chin. "I'm not going anywhere. I'll always be here to protect you."

Entwining my arms around his neck, I rise on my toes to kiss his perfect lips, the lips that formed the words, words a protector like him, a hero, means with all his heart. With my fingers now in his hair, the tips of our tongues meet, sizzling on impact.

"When's your game again?" I ask when the requirement for air takes us over.

"I'd say we have a few more minutes to spare."

Getting dressed, again, is somehow hilarious to the both of us. Perhaps due to the rush we find ourselves in after getting a little overzealous. Somehow, I managed to do to Shan what I never wanted to do to Derrick, and damn was it a turn-on. I didn't think doing *that* would have been as satisfying for me as it was for him; then again, I've never been turned around like that either. That position allowing our mouths to fully explore each other's sex, though I forgot what I was doing some of the time. He was a bit distracting down there.

Our eyes slide back and forth between concentrating on getting dressed and stealing looks at each other. I don't think my cheeks have stopped flaming, and I am pretty sure these untamed curls are a lost cause. Curls drape down my face in a swirling curtain of brown as I tie my shoes again. Derrick had always asked me why I didn't want to go blond. Seeing as most of his conquests when we were together were blond, I am thinking he picked the wrong girl from the get-go. Not-so-lucky me.

Sated and with an added layer of protection nearly wrapped around me from Shan's words and our physical manifestation of them, I head out the door with my head held high. I don't jump, not really, when Shan's arm wraps around my waist followed by a gentle squeeze. His head moves slowly as he sweeps the area; not a ripple of anxiety exists in the motion. No, this is smooth confidence personified.

My shoulders release a hidden stress, and I melt into his hold. I don't care who sees me with Shan. I'm proud to be with him, and he has shown me nothing but compassion and...

And what? Love?

Maybe love. Maybe that's what I am feeling as well, but can a broken and untrusted heart fall so quickly? And if so, should I trust it all completely? I've been wrong—*so* wrong—before.

Not this time.

Shan opens Tyler's car door and I slide in, carefully eyeing the oddities I toss aside and avoid. Boys can be so gross.

I don't see eyes, and I try to hold onto my unwavering carelessness about who sees me with Shan, but a sensation of them burning into me slips through the cracks of my old habits and fears.

It's just your imagination. Shake it off.

I refuse to look around. Why should I care?

"So, I will talk to you later tonight?"

"Absolutely," I promise. "I want to hear all about the game. I'll be studying at Nia's, but text me."

A shadow plays along his face as we pass the thick line of trees on our way to my dorm. The sun shines more fully, yet a shadow is still there. Is he worried?

We pull into my parking lot, and I gather my purse to me, nearly hugging it like a favorite blanket. I notice I'm looking down again, and Shan's words come back to me about not feeling ashamed of my past, so I pull my shoulders back and out of my slump.

"You're worried." My statement holds more power than if I had asked it as a question. I knew the answer to that already. Shan must think Derrick is still a threat. I know it.

"Do you have anything for protection when you go out alone? I know you can walk or drive to Nia's, but either way, do you have something?"

My hand slips into my purse and I pull out the bright pink holder with police-grade Mace inside.

"It's one of the first things they had us decide on in the self-defense class my group took together." My hand holds out the small object that packs a punch. "These don't hurt either."

Shan's eyes widen at the set of knuckles attached to my keys like a painful promise. Bright purple coloring with lethal, sharp ears complete the kitty look of the dangerous weapon.

"Cute," he says as the shadow lifts away. "I feel much better knowing you have these."

"Yeah, so do I."

"Last night—well today, too, all of it was amazing." His words are followed by a touch to my knee that travels up my leg.

"Hey, you. No fair! We can't start this again or you'll miss your game." The flush in my cheeks is back again, but he doesn't push it, another way he is sexier and more of a man than my ex.

When his hand slides away, I shift toward him, instead touching his face with my hand and pulling myself closer one last time.

"You're a magnificent distraction, April."

"You're quite a diversion yourself, Mr. Carp."

I break away with a pout and hop out of the car. With a wave, I turn toward my hall, only to swivel around to see him waiting there, smiling while I walk away like a little girl who just got everything she asked for on Christmas Day.

It is nearing five, and I need to get something to eat before I meet with Nia. She already has a dinner plan with her newspaper group, and having just joined, she doesn't want to miss it no matter how looming this damn chemistry test may prove to be.

Aware of the lack of food in our dorm apartment, I decide to head downstairs to grab something in the dining hall to go.

While deep in my decision-making process over different sandwiches or pizza options, a presence looms behind me.

"Saw you leaving idiot Shan's house this morning." Chas spews his hate long enough to send a heated breeze to the back of my ear. "Just so you know, I sent Derrick a nice picture of the two of you looking all cozy."

"And I care why?" I reply while continuing to move down the line, opting for pizza for now and a sandwich to bring to Nia's. We'll be there awhile.

"Why? Don't you think you should show him some respect? He treated you like a queen, and now you're showing your tits to some loser."

Gripping my tray tightly enough to bring white and a splattering of red blood vessels abloom on my knuckles, I try to take a deep breath before setting the tray down.

Spinning around slowly, I point my finger at Chas. "Move away from me, Chas. You're in my space and your mouth is in my ear, so *back off*!"

His shit-eating grin only brings my finger to curl inward, my short nails managing to feel like tacks piecing my skin.

"I said back up!"

This time Chas raises his hands in the air. "Look, psycho chick, calm down. You're making a scene."

"Oh, I'm making the scene? But you can come up behind me like some freak of a stalker and try to threaten me because your dick boyfriend can't leave me alone? He had his chance, but I guess once an abuser and a cheat, always one."

"You're a lying bitch. I should wash out your lying mouth with these fake-ass mashed potatoes and make you choke on them."

Breathe and don't back down.

"I'm not scared of you, Chas, or your master, Derrick. He kept me under his thumb for too long, kind of like he is doing to you now. Wake up! If you ever want to be a decent guy you should distance yourself from him, like yesterday. Otherwise, I feel bad for any girl who wanders into your webs."

I don't think Chas takes a breath for about thirty seconds while I glare into his eyes, not breaking our contact, not dropping my eyes to my hands, which are shaking in rage. My life is my own, and Derrick and his cronies aren't going to control what I do and whom I do it with.

"You don't know what you're talking about," he grits through clenched teeth.

"Don't I?" My head tilts while my lips purse. I pick up on a small drift of his eyes, as if he is actually considering my words.

I decide the standoff can end on my terms. Plus, I am famished. Smiling at him instead of holding onto my grimace, I turn around, grab my tray, and walk away. I don't look back. Even though I've held my ground, I am still trembling inside like a downed beetle, and any small movement might just unleash the tremors.

This getting back to who I was thing is complicated, because I don't think that person was ready to deal with this crap either. I keep saying Derrick made me weak, but something must have been missing in my confidence to begin with in order to let his wickedness leak into my psyche. I try not to let that beat me down. I mean what teenager is truly uber-confident? We are all just finding our way, both then and now, and when someone appears to love and cherish us, even a would-be protector cloaked in a deep-rooted guise, it can be easy to fall for the wrong person.

Not like Shan, right?

Trust is hard, people.

I scan my card and leave the cafeteria. I get nods and smiles from some of the other students who saw the interaction along with a couple glares from other soccer players and their hater girlfriends who know Derrick and believe he's a god. A false god is more like it. Why can't people find a better, less sinister and cowardly person to look up to? Of course, I was enamored by the star athlete as well, so who am I to judge? I guess the real question is, can I forgive and forget about what happened in our relationship? And on another note, do I ever think Derrick can change and become a better person? It's hard to see past the abuse, both physical and mental, or the lies, but maybe change is possible. Isn't that what we want in the world?

Realizing that I'm heading to my car lost in my thoughts, something I was told not to do at self-defense class, I snap out of it and pick up the pace.

"Where are you off to, sweetheart?"

The bile in my stomach shoots up my throat, burning the inside of my mouth.

Damn it, girl! You weren't paying attention.

I clutch my keys, shifting them to slip my knuckles into place. By moving to the side, I am now able to see Derrick, my car, and my hall at the same time.

"What do you want, Derrick? I have somewhere to be."

"Are you having another date with Shan?" He sneers. "Do you even know that guy? I mean, well enough to give it up already?"

Breathe, in out in out. Don't overreact. That's what he wants.

"I'd say I know a lot more about Shan than I ever really knew about you. Or maybe I was just a confused little girl who was blind to what you were really all about. Control, lies, and physical and mental abuse."

I've never said this out loud to him—only in texts when he wouldn't leave me alone once I found my voice in group and knew what it really was that he was doing to me nearly every day. No, I didn't need group to know the physical part was happening and that it was wrong, but to learn that all of the earlier mind games leading up to his carnal rage should have been warning signs all along that he was jacked. But I was in love, I trusted him, and sadly, at times I thought he was right and that I even deserved what he was saying to me. Maybe I was a flirt, or a tease needing attention and looking elsewhere. Which I was—at Shan.

These words rush through my head as I gauge his reaction. He doesn't flinch; though when does a stalking tiger flinch?

"I'm not the person you think I am. You're just being fed a bunch of bullshit from your cult lesbian group." He takes a step toward me and I tighten the grip on my deadly kitten knuckles. "I bet you didn't tell him all the things you did to me. How you provoked me. I don't get mad with anyone but you. Just you, April! Now explain that to me!"

Derrick's yell doesn't rattle me on the outside, but I am barely keeping it together inside.

"Maybe you did love me, once, but you need help, Derrick. When you do find love again, I fear this cycle will continue." I pull a smile despite the vehemence in my heart. "Maybe you can change."

"You're the one who needs to change. I'm just fine and everyone knows you're a liar."

"Not Shan."

"Oh, that's rich. If you think he'll ever love you like I did, you're wrong."

"I hope not, Derrick."

Uh-oh.

His steps are invisible to my ears, as if he floats to me.

"Back off, Derrick." I hold my knuckles by my side, my elbow locked and taut as a tightrope. His eyes glance down before moving back to mine.

"What are you going to do with that?" He laughs. "You'd never."

"Really, like you'd never destroy someone's property. Smart thing spray painting the cameras."

Good, throw him off guard.

"What in the hell are you talking about?"

His eyes widening and a drop in his jaw make me wonder if Shan was right. No, it had to be him.

"You're trying to tell me you didn't dump paint all over Shan's car when we were on our date last night?"

He takes a step back and then another. Changing the subject, kind of, seems to have worked. He's too conceited not to want to know what people are thinking of him, especially if law enforcement, or the college, could be involved.

"I don't know what you're talking about, April." His arms cross and his mouth sets to a sideways sneer. He's shut off to me now. Something I remember fondly.

It's hard to tell with this Derrick if he truly doesn't know because he didn't do it, or if he's wanting to play his brain-screwing games with me just to keep me entwined with him somehow.

"I guess we'll see. I'm sure they'll figure out who is behind it soon enough."

His side smirk moves, without a shift in his eyes, to the other side with a touch of his nasally laugh just for fun.

"It's been nice seeing you, April. Say hi to Nia for me."

Time to go.

Without turning around, I slip around to the driver's side of my car and get inside to the echo of sliding locks.

What a dick.

"Such a dick."

Does he know where you're going?

I wouldn't put it past him, though Nia is friends with people that are a few degrees separated from those who report to Derrick, and it's not like I can be in a witness protection program. Derrick has to let this go soon. Of course, if he's insane enough to commit a crime…

Another crime.

Yes, I can report his abuse. I feel bad enough about unleashing him on the world without notifying the proper authorities, but like I said, I've already been warned, in not so many words by more than one of the soccer coaches, to keep my mouth shut. Though they tried to come across as being supportive, I know better now. Once deceived by one snake, the others are easier to beat out of the grass.

Maybe it is time to talk to someone on campus or at the station. Especially if he screwed with Shan's car. I'm sure Shan will list him as a suspect, right? Is Derrick really that dumb?

He thinks he can get away with anything, remember?

I get to Nia's and push the stick into park. I don't think I took one true breath all the way over here, not with all the rear and side mirror viewing and peeking for my ex's car. No one followed me into the lot. With the tension easing from my neck, my head flops back against my headrest followed by a long series of deep inhales and exhales.

This isn't normal. Why can't I just have a chill, normal life? Why did I let this happen? Salty wetness prods at the corners of my eyes, hot and stinging as if a bitter smoke came shooting out of my car vents hell-bent on yanking tears from my eyes. I don't hold back; why should I? The emotions of the past twenty-four hours release from each side of the spectrum. My mind cycles from the highs of my date with Shan to the fear at what happened to his car, but then that was quickly dampened by our time back at his house. Just thinking about it warms my body and fights away some of the sadness.

Derrick's shade may have reemerged multiple times afterward, whether from by my own worry or when facing Chas, before he showed in true form moments ago, making me fear for my safety outside my dorm. I knew that leaving my ex wouldn't end things for good, but it's been months now. Why can't he just let me go?

He wants to control everything, and you aren't letting him do what he wants. How many times do you think he hasn't gotten his way?

I'd say close to never.

Tears fall, even with the visions of Shan touching me, kissing me, telling me I am beautiful. They all drift away when my shit of an ex comes back to mind. I can't let him do this. I need to stop him for good.

Restraining order.

Yes. It's time.

Chapter 10

I Know

It seems like an hour of waiting passes by while I wait to speak to a campus officer before I finally leave, opting to get some advice from my group leader, Kathy, instead. Something didn't feel right as I sat there, like I was being put off. Like they knew why I was there and whom I was reporting. Now I'm not a conspiracy nut— okay, maybe a little—but I had been cautioned before, so who wouldn't be suspicious?

Said suspicions are confirmed when I spy the soccer coach marching across the campus lawn toward the security building as I slip behind a tree. I am in over my head here, stuck in a circle of lies and cover-ups, just like Nicole Bends, Shan's mother.

At that, I run. I run harder than I can remember ever running before, but maybe that's because my feet seem to be digging into rocky mud or nearly hardened cement. Regardless of if my mind is playing tricks on me or not, I'm back in my room, kneeling in front of my toilet before I even realize I've made it that far.

"What am I going to do?"

Tears come next. Followed by the creaking of the door and a "Hello? April."

Oh shit, Shan.

Shooting my foot out, I slam the bathroom door closed with a wince. My muscles scream at the sudden awkward movement and the lactic acid built up in their fibers.

"Sorry, I didn't mean to just walk in. I saw the door open and I got...well, I figured you were just chilling." Shan's response to a door literally being slammed in his face can be read like a book.

Well, he's not wrong. Something is up.

"I-I just need a minute," I say between silent gasps of air. Air to push down my rising nausea and unease.

"I can leave if this isn't a good..."

"No," I yell, interrupting him. "No, please stay. I'll be right out."

What choice do I have—I mean, really? Either way, he's going to be put off. Somehow. Someway. At least this way I have some control.

When I come to standing, the reflection that greets me doesn't find my choice to be a good one.

Whoa, your hair. Your shirt. Your...

"Okay, I get it." My teeth clamp down on my lip before I can talk to myself some more.

"What was that?"

"Nothing," I sing.

I need to get myself together, bring all of those pieces of me that were scattered by the raw realization that control and power win over truth. The power of the athletic department, of the soccer team, of Derrick's money, it all matters more than what one girl has to say about the horrors their prince has bestowed upon her behind closed doors. At least the doors were closed, and no one saw. But that also means that there isn't any proof.

But there is.

The eyes in the mirror freeze, refocus, and then a furrow in my brow smooths to allow my eyes to narrow.

With newfound realization coming to light, I get my shit together. By shit, I mean my askew hair and crumpled clothes, and my diminished posture. I mean I did just have my face hovering over the sickening fumes of the dorm's john. With one hand in my hair and the other in my vanity drawer, I manage to make myself look more presentable. But it isn't the lip gloss or the pin in my hair that makes me feel ready to face Shan; it's the power glittering behind my eyes—the determination. Of course, brushing my teeth is a close second.

Reaching for the door, I take one more breath to prepare to see the man I may now be in love with, a man who shows adoration, not ownership.

"Okay, all good. How are you?" My smile finds him easily. His back is to me while he looks out my window along the wall that lines my bed.

"I'm good. How about you?" His turn toward me continues into a stride. "Seriously, I'm sorry about just showing up. I know that can be unnerving."

He thinks he scared me.

"I should know better than to leave that door open. I just got a little jumpy." Why am I saying that? To make him think I'm still that frightened girl who can't take care of herself? "Wait, that's not entirely true."

Take a deep breath and just tell him.

"It's been a long twenty-four hours," I start. "Last night, on my way to Nia's, Derrick was waiting for me near my car. Nothing happened, and I'm fine, but then today…"

"Did he hurt you?" His hands meld into fists by his sides, followed soon after by a quiver in his jaw. He stopped about two feet from me, and I hate the distance, but don't step closer.

"No, and today I went to talk to the campus police about what he had done to me, to make a report, but it didn't go well."

"What happened?" The trembling stops and his fists relax, but I can still see a muscle bulging in his jaw. His gorgeous jaw.

Focus.

"After being left to wait it out for an hour, I took off. I could tell they were blowing me off." My anger tries to bubble over again. "When I was leaving, I saw the head coach raging toward the building. They were going to toss anything I said into fire and stomp on the charring remains."

Oh my, you didn't.

I have zero tact sometimes.

"Elitist bastards!" Shan seethes. "They think they can control everything and everyone. I've seen it firsthand."

Way to scrape open old wounds, April. But really, who truly forgets going through something like that?

"I know you and your family went through something similar, and I hope this isn't upsetting you." This time I do force away the distance between us to wrap my fingers around his hands. "But I have another idea. I'm not going to be quiet. I need to warn others about Derrick. If I can save one woman from falling into his trap, then this will all be worth it."

His hands squeeze mine, and I look up to see him swallow as if his throat is as dry as a summer desert.

His jaw relaxes soon after and he looks down at me with that delicious smile.

"I'll help you any way I can, if you'll let me."

"Of course. I just wasn't sure if you'd want to deal with something like this after everything you've been through with your mom."

"I want to, for you." He pulls me closer and my ear touches his chest, his rapid heartbeat pleasing me at first, before shooting doubt into my mind.

"Are you hungry?" His question is muffled through his chest.

"Are you here for the food?" I ask with a laugh before breaking from our hug to look into his eyes. Eyes tell the truth.

His seem to see only you.

But there was also a crease I haven't seen before in his grin. Before I can let my mind go to town on my worries, he pulls me off my heels and kisses me with a passion and a need so intense I forget to think or breathe.

"I'm here for you, and the food. In that order."

I swat him playfully.

"I mean there's a huge gap between you and the food. Hey."

I dance away from him teasingly, turning my back on him and giving a sway to my hips. His answering, chuckling growl prods me to move faster, but not enough to keep him from grabbing ahold of my hips and spinning me toward him again.

"Food can wait, you know. I don't see a roommate at the moment."

"What roommate?" I giggle, lost in the moment, in his smell and touch.

He lifts me, carrying me to my bed. As his lips and body lower to mine, any doubts I have are swept away by kisses and caresses of warm fingertips upon my skin.

***

Watching Shan take down three helpings of pasta and meatballs is quite a sight. The first one didn't seem to faze him as he excused himself for seconds, but halfway through the third, he gave me an adorable boyish grin before twirling his fork again.

"You aren't hungry?" he asks between swallows. He has his manners still, despite his destruction of food. "Or isn't it good?"

There is that crease again, something tugging back on his face that signals something more.

"I was, but I think the protein in that shake caught up with me and my eyes were bigger than my stomach." Or, despite the touching and holding and kissing mere minutes ago, it has only diluted my worries. "What's your week look like?"

After running through what we both have going on leading up to spring break, it is clear that neither of us has solid plans on what we are doing for the week. He plans on heading off to see his mom for some portion of it, and I am seeing my family.

"I'll call you later, okay?"

"That's more than okay," I reply softly, placing my arms on his shoulders and lifting to plant a kiss on his cheek. "Thank you for coming to see me. It was a nice surprise."

Cue the crease. Followed by the grasping of my waist into a soft, firm hug.

"I miss you when I'm not with you," he says.

"I miss you, too."

We say our goodbyes, not having spoken about Derrick during lunch. Shan wanted to know about my plan back in my room, but I think he's too close to everything that's happening. I can't release that gnawing feeling in the back of my mind, and I've already brought his dark memories tiptoeing back—or rather raking and clawing back—into the forefront of his mind.

Really, though, why am I giving myself that much credit?

It's more likely that the reality of his past, of his mother's past, is always hovering there, always tipping him one way or the other. It's a cycle between pain and regret before settling into some sort of acceptance and gratitude that his mother is alive and that her torture is over. Torture from his own flesh and blood.

How do you reconcile with that?

Shame comes fleeting between the pathways of my thoughts. Doesn't Shan need support and compassion as much as I do, if not more? What's been happening instead is that he's been taking care of me, worrying about how I am when his life has been broken in more places than mine. It hasn't been long since we began this relationship together, so I'm not going to push him to talk about it if he's not ready. Maybe he doesn't want to, ever, and maybe he really is okay. Years have passed since his traumatic experience took place, and I'm sure he's had someone to lean on, right? Of course, I could be wrong, and everything is just as raw and bitter as the night he saved his mom from his sadistic father. And the abuse itself? That had gone on for years. Does time ever allow someone to truly move past it all?

Has he healed enough to have my story in his life without dragging it all back?

The new crease in Shan's smile flickers to life in my memory, and I stumble on my next thoughts. Could that mean he needs to talk about what happened to him with my new course of action breaking open the wounds, or at least causing their previous trickle to gush open and destroy the haphazard bandage that once held back the tidal wave of hurt? The least I can do is leave him out of what I have to do next. Regardless of how close to the surface his past is to his present, why would I bring him any closer to something that can trigger something more, something worse, or cause him to walk away from us?

With my decision made, I call Nia instead and we decide to meet up at a little coffee shop, somewhere we've never been in case tabs are still being kept. We find our way to the back, by the reading section lined with bookshelves and hidden nooks. How have we not come here before?

I unfold a couple pieces of paper I kept hidden within the slot of an old folder, where the cardboard of a legal pad would slide in. I've never shown them to anyone, but I've told Nia and my support group about their contents. Those story-tellings were from pure, rote memory, since I haven't actually looked at them at all recently. Regardless, here's my proof. Proof of threats upon paper by Derrick himself, telling me what he would do—to me, to someone else, to even himself—if I didn't do what he said. Sometimes that meant not breaking up with him, other times that meant not hanging out with any of my guy friends, and sometimes that meant I had to forgive him for what he had done. Though he's really never admitted to doing anything in the first place, so his idea of forgiving him was by truly telling me to get over it and to stop acting paranoid.

Derrick would always tell me he was raised to always lie, even if you did something wrong.

"If somebody comes up to you and asks you about something you did, you lie," he'd say, "and then you lie again."

My ex is the master of lies. At least at first, but then after a time it was very obvious to me when he had been doing something unfaithful, which actually turned out to be nearly all of the time he went out without me. Every time he drank, or a girl showed more interest in him than friendship, he'd pounce. I don't doubt that every weekend he went out without me, another girl was involved. I know Derrick wanted me to want only him, but to my ex, I was never enough. Perhaps he has a void that just can't be filled with just one person. Maybe he's less confident than he portrays. That's what we've learned in group. Abusers control, and they do the exact thing they accuse us of doing because their needs can never be fulfilled. They can never satisfy the attention they didn't get or longed for in the past, but they keep trying, and at anyone else's expense.

"These are awful, April, but I am so glad you kept them." Nia's fingers push aside one note and then another as if she's touching something grotesque or perhaps sharp enough to draw blood. "Are you scared?"

"I'm done being scared." This isn't a lie, so why does my stomach quiver? "Derrick used fear to keep me with him. He's not going to be able to use it to keep me from telling my story."

"You're so brave, April. I am glad you got away from that monster."

"That makes two of us."

I look around our new digs, wondering if Derrick has somehow put a tracker on me. I know this isn't the movies, and just because he was outside my dorm doesn't mean he's stalking me, right? Regardless if he's only done it once, or has been doing it all along, I can't shake the feeling, which is why I need help. Real help. Legal help.

After getting home, I call my group leader, Kathy, and sit on my bed taking notes, crying, and at times even cry-laughing while we go over my decision to file a restraining order against Derrick. I go to bed ready for action the next day. But something is nudging at my brain while I wrestle with my covers, trying to find that dark drop-off into sleep.

Shan.

When I roll over the next morning, I fumble along my bedside table until I find my phone. The dark screen refuses to reveal any notifications, so I toss it toward the end of the bed and flop my arm over my eyes. I had one missed call from Shan yesterday, which I returned unanswered, and after that—nothing. If we hadn't been communicating nonstop for over a month, I wouldn't give it a second thought, but that isn't the case.

There has been some talk about meeting each other's parents over spring break, and I wonder if that is still going to hold true. If I wasn't so tired last night, the worry may have kept me awake, but my soul was shaken preparing for the day, and nothing was keeping me away.

What I am going through must remind him so much of his mom and dad, and my broken record keeps thinking that he'd be better off with a girl that isn't slightly broken. He already has one of those in his life.

Of course, this could all be me creating uneasiness in my own head. I have plenty of concerns, but new ones have formed since my time with Shan—ones about losing somebody who is finally true and good and honest, but I'm not going to force it. The last time I did things and didn't do things for a guy, everything went to hell.

I need to do this for myself, for my safety, and for the wellbeing of the other girls who will cross Derrick's path. There's no doubting he's a tractor beam. He draws you in with an unbridled confidence topped with a gorgeous face and misleading chivalry. It would have been easier if he was a dick from the beginning. Maybe then things would be different.

The reality is, if my life, and the steps I am choosing to take, trigger Shan too much, he may be better off finding somebody who doesn't have some of the same baggage that he and his mother share. Baggage is a lame word, an understatement, to describe what his family is carrying, especially her. I'm flying solo here; she has her kids watching and learning from what unfolded. Luckily that cycle was broken, and Shan didn't become his own version of his father. What I escaped is nothing like what Nicole endured. In knowing that, I wouldn't blame him. I knew the first time he laid eyes on that bruise Derrick left around my eye that I reminded him of something horrible. Yet I've grown from that girl who took shit. A girl who didn't stand up for herself and put a guy first.

So here I am, poised to enter the police station near the courthouse to meet with an officer about filing a restraining order. A female officer is meeting me here—just one of the many things I requested and prepared after my time with Nia and call with Kathy. I already made copies and took photos of everything I have, which is something I'd do no matter what, regardless if I trusted the system or this officer to not lose, tear, or "accidentally" destroy the evidence before copies could be made. This isn't Shan's mother's town, but it is a small college town so there's a risk in everything I'm about to do—which is why I'm recording this entire conversation because there's no way I'm letting this go down without a fight.

Speaking of fights, little did I know Nia snapped a photo of my face when it was covered in painful hues of black and blue. She had intended to show it to me if I thought giving Derrick another chance was a nifty idea. It was hard for her to show me, and equally hard for me to look at, but I'm glad she did, and for the reason she did, even if it meant she had little faith in my conviction at the time. Nia had cause; I have already gone back to Derrick too many times and after too many shitty things.

"I wasn't going to show anyone," she said back in the coffee shop. But she also knew a lot about the female officer I should speak to and what the process would be like for me, so I had a feeling she was going to go for me if I tried to stay with my abusive ex-boyfriend.

"You're a good friend, Nia. Smart and sneaky as hell too. Remind me not to cross you." I laughed before we hugged across the distance between us. I don't know what I would do without her or the support I get from group.

My family doesn't know any of this yet, and I am hoping my report doesn't wrap them into it more than they need to be. They don't need to worry about me when they live on the other side of the state. They'd come down here right away if they knew, and even though I love them, they'd try to get me to come back home. Being their sheltered daughter may have been part of why Derrick snuck me into his web of lies in the first place, and I don't want them to come to this realization the way I have and blame themselves for what's happened. Though, thinking about it now, it's something I should talk to them about with my little sister, who's still living at home. Of course, they've never been able to keep Laura as locked down as I was, but maybe that's because she's smarter than me, like she always claims she is.

Officer Karen Simmons is an irreplaceable woman to have on my side. Not only is she knowledgeable on domestic abuse and violence, she's also brought in a lawyer friend of hers, who is happily meeting with both of us to go over the restraining order paperwork. This is the first step, and hopefully the only one we need, to push Derrick in the right direction before taking it further and pressing charges. I have a good deal of proof that should lead to the courts upholding the restraining order, but it's a much bigger course of action to take Derrick to court for abuse. The restraining order is my ex's warning shot across the bow, and, as Karen and her friend Maggie hope, the judge will be recommending counseling for Derrick at the hearing.

The idea of having to attend a hearing with Derrick causes my throat to close slightly, as if a hot and bitter liquid is gluing the sides together. I move to open a nonexistent top button from my blouse, opting to guide my hands to my jeans instead. A small trail of my fingers' marks changes the coloring of my pants to a darker blue.

"I'll come with you, if you like. Pro bono, of course," Maggie offers kindly as she sits next to me in the worn conference room chair at the station. "We've been looking into the lack of follow-through on your campus with a variety of assault issues. If you don't mind, I think we can help each other." She uncrosses her cream-colored pantsuit-covered legs and leans forward to touch my hand. I accept the gesture and let her take my hand. She gives me a reassuring squeeze and a smile, one that lights up her eyes where they sit above high cheekbones and are framed by her short, curly onyx hair, which shines in the blinking halogen lights.

I nod to both women who have somehow joined me to create a team to not only go after Derrick, but to make changes at Crimson State as well. The two women are perfect complements to each other. Karen sits on the table with her bright red hair pulled back, startling against her dark blues eyes and contrasting with the ass-kicking gear attached to her belt.

"I'd be lying if I told you I wasn't nervous about backlash, but it won't keep me from going forward," I declare. "Especially now that I have the both of you."

"We will be with you every step of the way," Karen promises.

Neither of the women showed surprise when they heard my retelling of what happened—or didn't happen—when I went to campus security for help.

"A shakedown has been a long time coming," Maggie reveals. "And if we can get Judge Darlin, like I hope, the case we've been building will be getting the extra support it needs. Your campus needs a rude awakening."

I swear I hear Maggie's knuckles crack like she's preparing for a fight. Karen must have heard it, too. Her freeing laugh in Maggie's direction gives us a nice distraction from the seriousness of the situation. For a moment at least.

"I just hope Derrick gets the hint and does what he's supposed to do." I can't trust anything he may do. "Not only is he still bothering me, but I think he trashed my friend's car as well."

Just your friend?

I'm not sure why I omitted boyfriend. I suppose I don't want them to think this isn't a big deal, and would they indeed feel that way knowing I've moved on? Or is it actually the trickle of doubt running from my toes up to my neck and back again since Shan may not even be that, or want that, after all?

"Oh, I think he'll behave," Maggie interjects, assuring me with her no-nonsense tone. "He doesn't have the school protecting him in this matter. They'll need to help him comply or things are going to get even messier."

I nod to Maggie, but not without noticing Karen gnawing on her cheek.

"I don't mean to worry you, April." Her jaw stops moving, and she reaches for the same hand her friend once held. "Maggie and I have worked closely together over the last year after realizing what's been happening on campus, on many campuses, but we hit some walls here at times as well."

"Let me handle that one, Karen." The two women look at each other, something passing between the friends. It's silent but powerful. "I've tapped into their system of handing off or losing these sorts of things in their red tape, but there are more of us on our side than anyone realizes. Some who have gone into the trenches just to get the proof we need to oust many of the conspirators. It's only a matter of time," Maggie hints with a wink in my direction. "It also helps that my brother is in internal affairs, and unlike some siblings, we talk all of the time."

"This is bigger than I ever thought it was. I mean, I see this stuff on social media and on TV, but there were honestly times I thought I was just making it up in my head, just being paranoid, you know?" Both Maggie and Karen nod at me, their smiles cycling between knowing and wishful.

"I wish it was only a tale of fiction," Karen muses. "But art truly does imitate life, and in these cases, it's unfortunate."

Maggie stands to give Karen a hug and me a supportive squeeze on my shoulder. "We'll be with you every step of the way, girl. If your poster boy for the soccer team knows what's good for him, he'll comply, and he'll bust his butt to change as much as he does when he's playing with his ball."

We all laugh as she walks away, leaving Karen and I to make a trip next door to the courthouse to finish and submit the paperwork before saying our goodbyes as well.

"He'll be served soon, so prepare for a little backlash if he's as reactive as you say. I wish I didn't have to give you that warning, but many abusers react the same way when they're provoked."

Her half smile holds tension in her cheeks, reminding me of the crease in Shan's eyes. He still hasn't called or texted.

"Between this and what may come down about your friend's car, he's going to be steaming in a bath of, pardon my French, deep-shit water."

Good.

"I wonder if Shan will report it to the police. I only know that he called his insurance agent. I doubt he'd want to just let it go and pay for it all himself, but he's been involved in a cycle of abuse before, and he may not want to go there again."

"Does he know everything?" she asks, sympathy softening her eyes. I don't think she bought the "friend" bit before.

"Not all of it," I reply before shaking my head, reminding myself not to let it fall in shame. "But what happened to his mom is truly terrible, and I think I may be reminding him too much of the fire and his dad."

"Wait, is his mother Nicole Bends? The woman whose husband set the fire, killing himself and nearly taking her with him?" Her eyes are wide, both astonished and sad. "Her son saved her life."

I can only nod—barely, the weight of my dejection and defeat making the movement difficult. Shan doesn't need any more of this in his life. He's already faced it enough, more than anyone should ever have to.

"My God, April. I can't imagine how difficult it must be for you all to deal with this Derrick situation. Ms. Bends' case is brought up to all of the new trainees when we discuss domestic abuse and ethics." Her hands come to her hips, the belted weaponry and her stance giving her the air of a worthy advisory. "Those officers dropped the ball big time. Even Maggie's brother was brought in on the case after all of the mishandlings in that jurisdiction's internal affairs office. So tragic."

"Have you ever met her?"

Karen shook her head.
"She's a fighter."
"So are you."

Chapter 11

Reflections & Reminders

Though I am relieved to have finally put pen to paper, having set into motion something that will both make Derrick take some responsibility and hopefully lead toward change, or at least a clear warning that he is dangerous, I'm unnerved. That and a little scared.

Yesterday was both exhilarating and exhausting. Karen and Maggie are amazing, but the unknown clambers around my brain like a thief or a hell-bent ninja. Nia was on edge as well, asking me, more like demanding me, to move in with her for a while. Agreeing with her concern, I began packing a bag of clothes, books, my laptop, and anything else I could think of. It was a bizarre state of packing.

My roommate sits in our room either ignoring me completely or just staring. "So, yeah, are you sure you're cool with Bobby staying here while you're gone?" Her question, though directed at me, is spoken into her fingernails she pretends to find issue with. "I mean you should be since it's your psycho ex-boyfriend that's giving us the wrong sort of feels, ya know."

"I'm totally sure, Heather. That's why I told you and suggested this very thing. I don't want my crap to impact you."

Heather, my specter of a roommate, stays at her boyfriend Bobby's most of the time anyhow, but according to her, his roommates are childish. I swear she came here looking for a husband, not a degree.

The eye roll she gives me makes me want to take back my concern for her, and perhaps break a nail or two. The thoughts and images of doing someone harm aren't things I'd ever act on, but having been on the other side of such violence, I shudder at the thought of that thin line, the sheer veil, that keeps us from that vicious choice. When does a person's conscience finally step aside and let the primitive mind take over to do and take what it wants?

My shiver earns me another look, or maybe it was an eye roll.

"You *could* put on some more clothes."

She's just the best. Ugh.

There's no sense in responding; I learned that early on in the semester.

"I'll text you Nia's information in case you need to get ahold of me for anything."

Thumbs-up, zero eye rolls this time.

"Okay, well, take care and I'll be in touch."

The walk to my car is uneventful, though my eyes dart left and right, searching for any signs of payback from my ex, if he's gotten served already. I doubt the clunky wheels of justice motor this fast, but I am tense in anticipation of anything and everything.

My car looks normal, no messages or pouring of paint to match Shan's. I do plan on calling him once I get to Nia's. He should know my course of action from my own mouth and not in a text—that's just how it needs to be done.

The drive is uneventful as well, and when I get to Nia's house, she graciously opens the door with a beaming smile on her face, something Heather has never and would never do.

"Got everything you need? I mean it isn't like you can't go back and get it, but, well you know."

"Yep, everything I'll need for a few days. Hopefully I won't have to crash at your place longer than that," I reply.

"You can stay as long as you want. I'm just glad I agreed to take my parents' old, clunky pull-out couch so you have something decent to lie on." Nia's gaze shifts to the gray, worn but comfy couch in the living room. "It already has sheets on it, so it'll be ready to go when we pull it out. I can grab your other stuff for you."

"Thanks, my comforter is in there still and my other bag." I sound so blasé when I need to sound more appreciative. I hate imposing on others, but this is one of those once-in-a-lifetime things, and Nia is a true friend. Another thing that doesn't come around very often, but the good kind.

"I need to call Shan," I call to her since she has already snagged my keys and bolted to my car. "Can I use your room?"

"Of course," she hollers back while closing my trunk, though my fluffy cover muffled most of it.

I find Shan's name and hover my finger over the telephone icon, hesitating to initiate the call. It's been nearly two full days, and nothing. I know what that means.

This doesn't mean it's over, you know. He could just be busy.

Maybe, but I doubt it. Chances are more likely that he came to his senses. Maybe I should come to mine too. What am I doing anyhow? Jumping to a new boyfriend after everything I've been through? Probably not the smartest plan, but whose heart is ever that clever anyhow?

After my eyes glaze over from their intense stare, I press the button, listening as the tinkly ring mimics the blinking screen.

"Hey. How are you? Sorry, I've been meaning to call you back." His rushed words are what I want to hear, but the tone is all wrong.

"It's okay," I lie. "I've been busy as well." I swallow as silently as possible, though the dry lump of words I don't want to speak is making it difficult. "I won't keep you long. I just really wanted, well, I really think you should know I filed a restraining order against Derrick with the courts yesterday."

Silence. One, two, what seems like one hundred seconds of painful, deafening silence.

"That's good. I'm glad you did, and I hope this gets his attention and that he leaves you alone for good."

What he doesn't say, not verbally, but I swear I can read his mind, is that he hopes it works out for me though it didn't for his mom.

"I hope so, too. Nia helped do some of the legwork for me, and I have some awesome women in my corner." I beam at the power of friendship and camaraderie. "I'm also staying here, at Nia's, for a while, just to make sure he doesn't overreact when they serve him"—*like he probably did with your car*—"you know, just in case you decide you want to hit up the cafeteria again. I won't be there for a few days."

"I go there for more than the food."

See.

"I know." I think.

There is a slamming door, and loud footsteps echo across our connection.

"Shan? Hey, man, it's all cleaned up and they're bringing us a new trashcan, so we're all good." Movement and a sound of motion come next. "Oh, damn, sorry man. I didn't realize you were on the phone. Is it? Never mind, sorry."

The same footsteps retreat, echoing my thoughts of my own escape. Something has happened. I can tell.

"What happened?" My breath comes in heaves. "Is this why I haven't heard from you? Something else happened, didn't it?"

Whoa, whoa, whoa.

But I don't care. I'm not going to let someone keep things from me, again, or blow me off. That April is long gone.

"It's nothing. Just some prank, I'm guessing."

"Another prank?" I seethe. "You don't really believe that, do you?"

"No one was hurt or in danger, really." His pause is telling. "We got to it quick."

"Got to what quick? Come on, Shan. You're dancing around this because you think it's Derrick, don't you?" How I wish my ex would stay the hell out of my life! "Did you ever tell the police you thought he did that to your car?"

"I can take care of Derrick," he responds coolly. "It was just a fire in the trashcan outside. It could have been the homeless needing some warmth, for all we know."

"Someone is messing with you, Shan. And a fire? After what happened?" I won't cry. I won't.

"Someone could have just tossed a butt in there. We aren't jumping to conclusions. We were home, so no harm done. We all agreed if someone wanted to really do some damage, they would have waited till there weren't any cars in the driveway."

His deep intake may have been to calm himself or out of exasperation for my concern. Either way, it sucks. I stay silent, with my jaw clenched so tightly I could start my own match between my teeth.

Another door slams and multiple footsteps follow the grating noise.

"Yo, are we doing this? We know where he is."

Now I stop breathing.

"Look, April, we're just going to talk to Derrick. Some of his teammates are helping us have a sit-down. It'll help resolve this crap and let him know to back off from you. I have to do something," he says in his protector voice. "As for the fire and the paint, I'm going to ask him about it, but there's also been chatter about other pranks with paint around campus, so I don't think I was targeted."

This would have all been nice to know, but instead I've gotten silence and right now it seems to have been either brushed off or more of a calm-the-hell-down-April vibe. I don't like either.

"Well, that's good," is all I can manage. The timing is still too coincidental for me, but Shan doesn't seem to agree—or maybe he doesn't care. If he backs away, which I fear he is, then this will all go away. For him, at least.

But he's trying to help you. He's telling Derrick to back off. He's protecting you.

Then why the radio silence?

"You'll be at Nia's for a while, right?"

Great small talk. "Yes."

"I'll give you a call later. Don't worry, seriously, things are under control."

"I hope so. I wouldn't want anything to happen to you." Again.

"And nothing will, to me or to you. That, I can promise."

The response is heroic and not the cool tone he had been giving me in his explanations. Maybe he was trying to keep calm for the both of us, and I'm the one overreacting.

Yeah, maybe you are reading this all wrong.

I have rights.

"I'll talk to you later then?"

"Yes, and April, you've done the right thing with the restraining order."

"Thank you. The court date won't be fun, but I don't mind facing him. He doesn't scare me." Anymore.

"I'll be right there!" he bellows to his invisible roommate. "I've got to run. I'll call you later."

"Okay."

"And April, you are amazing. You're everything I have ever wanted."

"You are too."

Goodbyes end the call, and my mind flips around inside of my head like a fish struggling to find some fount of water from the dock. What just happened and what is happening? Aside from his first statement about meaning to call me, he said nothing about the time he just took away from me, from us. Yes, it's early in the relationship, and two days may not seem like much, but when you've been all over each other over the phone and in person, it seems like forever.

Maybe he just needed some time to figure things out. He's obviously been working on things to help you. He is meeting with the asshat.

Speaking of asses, I don't believe this coincidence thing. Derrick is too controlling to not have been behind everything that's happening to Shan. First the paint that reminded me of flames dripping toward the pavement, and then an actual fire outside his house. He must have found out about his family and is using it to trigger Shan, to force him to react. How he'll react is the question. Will this "talk" lead to a fight, which Derrick can weasel out of and Shan won't? Or will it cause my new love to walk away from the sheer reminders of his terrifying past? Either option sucks big-time. I hate the thought of Shan suffering due to the correlations of my past with his own. While his is in the past, at least terms of time, mine continues.

He didn't seem to think he was battling his past. Only you do.

Maybe, but I've also learned to read people better.

Or maybe to mistrust them more.

Now that is possible, and one of the common responses to abusive trauma like mine. Yet I'm also not an idiot—not that Shan is, but I'm not going to ignore clear, flashing signs.

He isn't either.

Yes, he is going to meet with Derrick and his buddies. Pictures of his teammates flit through my mind. I wonder which ones have decided on this plan. The ones who were pretty cool weren't really friends with my ex. That should have been a clear signal. Dumb, dumb, dumb.

Not dumb, just blinded.

Right, and I am not letting that happen again. Instead, I am preparing for an end in sight for Shan and me. It's coming; I can feel it, and I don't blame him in the least. Maybe I should just end it first. Make the smart decision and let him off the hook. He didn't ask for any of this.

Neither did you, and he knew very well about Derrick before you even spoke your first words. Don't think for a minute he hadn't been scoping you out as much as you were him.

Shan didn't know the real nitty-gritty of it. He probably just thought Derrick was an asshole, which he is, but not everything he was doing. I mean, I will never forget his face and those words on the day he saw my eye.

"Those are the ones who can do the most damage," he said. "It's the ones who love them that change."

He may have thought I was less damaged when eyeing me from afar. Boy was he surprised.

You are not damaged.

But I don't trust love or my heart anymore. I don't trust that this will blow over. There's still too long of a jagged road to go.

I need to let him go.

But you don't know if that's what he wants.

This is not going to be about what some guy wants—not this time. It's going to be about what I want to do, need to do. I will trust these unruly, winged critters in my stomach this time.

He won't want to let you go.

109

It's not his decision. I won't be controlled. Not again. Not this time.

But don't you love him?

Tears burn, set afire like the paint streaking down Shan's car, which comes to life in my mind's eye. The picture changes to him racing into a burning house, carrying his mom in his arms to the screams of the evil monster who was left there to die.

He deserves happiness. This is only bringing the horror back.

Something like that never leaves you.

But you don't have to have a constant reminder, and I have myself to take care of. I can't worry about whether I'm hurting him or not all of the time.

It's too much.

And with that, I convince myself, and my other self, of what I should do. I am not sure what happened to that first inner voice. The timid one. The worried one. The one who didn't trust a thing.

Chapter 12

Break

Nia supports me with more than tissues. The chocolate keeps coming, as do the strong cocktails.

"Are you sure you want to do this?" she probes.

"I have to."

"But he said that things went well with Derrick," she pleads. "He doesn't think he did it. There was proof he wasn't at either place."

Yes, that may have been the case, but what didn't sit well was the text that explained all of this, not a phone call, and the subsequent brush-off after that, which kept him from calling or even messaging before.

"It's over, Nia. At least for now. I'm not going through this, and I can tell he's thinking the same thing." I sniffle. "It's best for both of us."

"Okay." She sniffles in response. She's a sympathetic crier. You should see her in movies or during commercials. "Are you ready?"

I've been staring at his contact name on my phone for an hour.

"No." I weep as my voice comes out as a croak. "But I have to."

The line rings and Nia shuffles back and forth on her bed trying to decide if she should come in close to listen or give me space. She stays at a distance, knowing she'll hear all about it afterward.

"Hi there." Oh, God, he seems happy. "I have been meaning to call you all day. Lab was crazy and so was practice."

What am I doing? Am I making a huge mistake? A false start on the blocks?

"It's okay. I just needed to talk to you really quick, if this is a good time."

"Yes, of course. What's up? Is everything okay?"

"I think it will be. For both of us." I swallow down my many winged flutterers once again and plow ahead. "I know this isn't the relationship you would have willingly chosen for yourself, and none of this is fair to you, so I think, I mean before it gets too serious, before one of us gets hurt, that we, that we…"

"April? Are you breaking things off with me? Everything is okay, really." Shan's rapid footsteps signal he's moving quickly, followed by a closing door. "I know I've been off lately, it was just hard for a couple of days, but it's okay, really."

Part of me wants to change my mind, but only for a second. It's been a sucky year with Derrick, and now that I am clawing my way out of this mess, I can't bring Shan along. This isn't only about protecting him; it's also about me—my heart. The one Derrick broke, and though it's been mending, I can't let it crack too deep along those scars by loving and losing Shan.

You do love him.

I think I have been falling in love with him for a while now. Before we even spoke.

"I've thought a lot about this, and please know this isn't easy for me." Not at all. "I know I'm triggering you and your distance from that is triggering me. We

112

are in a cycle and I can't, I just can't recreate confusion for me now. Not again."

"I'm not Derrick. I am not going to hurt you." His exhale is nearly a moan. "I'm sorry I've been distant lately. It's my fault. It won't happen again. I swear."

The words, from a different mouth, yet the same.

It's not the same. He's right. He's not Derrick.

I think we are on the same team now, and I'm still April, and I know myself, perhaps better than I ever have before, and this is just not the right time. It isn't anyone's fault.

"I am not blaming you. I'm not blaming myself either. It's the circumstances. It's my past mingling with yours. It's not good for either of us."

This sucks.

"Don't I have a say here? I know I screwed up, but this means so much to me. I...you mean so much to me."

I will not cry.

"And you to me. All I keep thinking is that things will get better after the court hearing, after the restraining order is issued, after Derrick leaves me alone, after this or that, but I can't settle myself if I keep hoping for more time to pass or by worrying about how this is hurting you."

"I can handle this. I want to. Just give me another chance. Give us another chance."

"Shan, look at what's happened so far. Your car. A fire. What if it gets worse? This is all because of me and you're acting like it isn't."

"It isn't..."

But I ignore him and keep driving ahead. My mind is set, and I won't ignore my worries or my gut again. "After what you and your family went through, this can't be something you want in your life. Not again. What would I say to your mom if I did come with you over spring break? I'm sure she knows all about me. Do you really think she wants this for her son? A girlfriend she already saw in a domestic violence support group?"

Dead Silence. Two deep inhales to calm myself, and then two more.

"She's excited to have you over. She even has another room for you to stay in so you can spend a few days with us." His shoes hit the floor at a quick pace, before pausing in what I assume is him turning and continuing in the other direction. "Will you at least think about it? Maybe just come for dinner one night?"

Just think about it, at least. You might learn something. It might help, plus you have nearly two weeks before break anyhow. That's lots of time to think.

"I'll think about it. But, Shan, if I do come, it needs to be just as friends, for now. It isn't only for you, though I care about you enough for it to be a big part of it. This is really for me. I need some time."

"I get it. I mean I don't want it to be this way, but I respect what you want." His voice cracks just enough to clench my lungs in mid-inhale. "I backed away, and I'm sorry. I knew I was doing it but didn't want to call it quits or push ahead without knowing if I could be what you need or if I could separate my past from our relationship. If it even makes a difference, and maybe it won't for now, but I want you to know that I do know. I know I want you. Every part of you. The healing parts, broken parts, the parts we don't even know about yet. All of you. When you're ready."

I don't even know when I started crying. The salty droplets plummet soundlessly and practically imperceptible in this heart-wrenching moment. All I

114

can focus on is breathing and not letting him know I am bawling over here, overflowing with emotion as tiny ocean-rivers leak from my eyes, drop from my lashes, and run along my cheeks down to my collarbone.

You love him.

Yes, but it isn't the time. He may think he knows, but he doesn't. He can't.

How can you be certain?

I'm not. But I'm also not ready for this love thing so soon, not yet. It hurt too much before.

"Thank you for understanding, and I am sor— I mean I know I must be making things so complicated for you." I will not apologize.

"You need to take care of you, and I get that," he replies. "You may not believe me, but I was getting ready to call you. I was just waiting on some information. I do think Derrick has gotten the picture. He was served, and from the sounds of it, the coaches are tired of covering his ass. Apparently, his parents just found out. They'd been kept out of the loop. His roommate overheard him talking to his mom and dad and he was bawling after. You did the right thing, April."

"I wish I could fall onto blind faith and believe the worst is behind me, but you don't know Derrick like I do." No one would want to. "When you met with him, what did he say exactly? Did he deny screwing up your car and the trash can fire?"

"He wasn't near either of those spots when it all went down. I don't think Derrick or his crew are lying. His guys were giving him serious heat about putting the team in jeopardy, but they're also his alibi." His pause wasn't for me to jump in just yet. "You were justified in thinking it was him. The timing was all there, plus he's a total dickhead, so why wouldn't it be him? But it looks like just some random crap, or at least the fire. The campus police are still looking into campus rivalry for the paint job on my car."

"That's good to hear." I sigh. What else can I say. I had been all spun up about what Derrick was doing to screw with this new relationship between me and Shan, and now I am left with a story unfolding that points to just coincidence and paranoia. On my part.

You have good reason—many of them…

"April, all of the signs pointed in his direction. I don't blame you for being suspicious. Hell, you may not have known it, 'cause I was trying to help and instead I ended up messing things up, but I didn't discount him either."

"I don't blame me either," I snap. "See, this is why I need a step back. Now I'm letting the fact that he didn't do anything impact us. I didn't mean to snap at you."

"I deserve it," he admits. "The word 'blame' is pretty much a cussword in my house. I don't always say the right things."

"It's okay. In time I won't be as sensitive, or mistrusting. You deserve that, Shan."

"So do you. Think about dinner, please? We are friends, you know, and as my friend I would love you to meet my mom and my sister, Clara. She'll be home from school," he says with a sudden lightness to his voice. "It's been forever since I've seen her, and she's been wanting to meet you."

Clara doesn't come home much, deciding to attend a high school abroad for a semester after their father died. The semester turned into a year and then another.

"Just give me a while to think. I also need to figure out my time at home as well." I thought I was decided,

116

but I hesitate, not wanting to let Shan go for good. "What night would you want me to come for dinner? My drive is five hours to get home."

"Yeah, I remember. Clara will be home before break starts, but has to return before it's over, so maybe before you go you can come by? It's only about an hour away. Though I know it's in the wrong direction for you."

"Okay, I'll let you know." My tears have become itchy, dried rivers of salt along both sides of my face. "Thank you for understanding. I don't want to close the book on us; please know that. I just need to close another one first. Something I should have done a long time ago."

"I understand, and I'm here for you. I always will be. And please believe me, even though I failed to prove it to you before, I can handle anything that comes *our way* with Derrick." He bites off the "k" like grit hit his teeth. "I won't turn my back on you because of what happened to my family. I promise you. I hope you can believe that so you're left with at least one thing you can set aside while you take the time you need."

"Okay," I answer shakily. "Thank you."

"I really am sorry, for all of it. I was a jerk and I took too long to figure that out."

"Thank you," I manage.

"Goodbye, April. I respect your space, but I'm not going anywhere."

"Okay," I squeak. "Goodbye."

Tears reignite the dead sea on my skin. I barely mange to press the *end* button before my body is racked with sobs and heaves, nearly unnaturally so, from deep inside my being. I've never felt like this before. The pain of not having what I want—not because I couldn't have it, but because I was protecting myself from it—is excruciating. Is it logical? It doesn't matter. What has to happen is something I didn't let happen before. I will build myself first, consider myself first, and if Shan is still there when I'm finally whole, then I will unleash this love breaking apart inside of me. I will knit it back together, piece by piece, and I will give it to him when I am ready, and when I know his ability to give me time, space, and to do the same for himself proves he is really able to do this, and that my past won't haunt both of us forever.

Is spotting a liar a super power? If so, I need some spandex and a mask, stat. The man sitting across from me, across from his massive desk that puts both actual space and arrogant space between him and anyone sitting across from him, looks more like a slick businessman than a dean of a public college. Oh, his words sound right on, just like his choice of vest, suit, and tie are all spot-on, but it doesn't make the look and sound of things appealing. On the contrary, I can't help the curl of my nose coming from a smell I can't place at first, but the vulgar tingling triggers my super powers, and I know instantly it's the stench of lies. He continues to talk, and I let it flow in and out of me, like a wave of deception slithering across my body and spilling out behind me. It doesn't stick, I'm not sold, and the bead of sweat on his brow proves he knows it as well.

Dean Harnett. The cad. The great deceiver. And perhaps the soon-to-be ex-dean if everything I've been privy to over these past ten days comes to fruition.

It all began with an odd mixture of phone calls and this dastardly meeting leading up to a much-needed spring break. From the school counseling center to the athletic department, it was a barrage of questions I didn't answer, per Maggie's instructions. She wasn't taking any chances with a possibility of manipulation or coercion—without her presence, that is. She'd love to catch them all in the act so she can find some heads to roll.

Though the dean's office was adamant they weren't aware of what was happening in their athletic department, let alone their campus security, Maggie and Karen weren't giving them any slack, unless it could be used for them to slowly unravel and hang themselves. Coach Banner appeared to be the scapegoat in all of this, the soccer coach appearing to be the most involved, but not with the most to lose.

It was this meeting in Dean Harnett's office that we accepted, after the third time they requested one. Maggie decided it might be a good way to record any admission of neglect to take with us to the court. Though the dean was, instead, evading his guilt and throwing the book at his coach, a man he claims has fooled him and vows it would never happen again.

"Do you know how many reports of assault have been made on Crimson State's campus over the last two years, Dean?" Maggie asks.

"Oh, I'm sure I can get that number from somewhere. Helen?" His holler is cut short.

"No need, Dean. We have that information here. It's three hundred cases." This causes a twitch to unleash in the dean's left eye. "And do you know how many of the reports have led to any action, of any sort, by the school?"

"Helen!"

Maggie slides a document across the table. "Five, sir. Five, and those weren't even the ones with the most violent of accusations." Maggie stands and puts her hand on my shoulder as a signal to rise as well. "You've done more than let Derrick Tinn harass one young woman. You've let many of your students down. And, Dean, we're coming for you."

"Helen!"

Helen isn't coming. She's been the leak to the two badass women on my side, on the side of justice, and she's getting ready to start her new job with Maggie's firm.

"A woman who can put up with what's been happening in this college and continued to play their game to help us nail their asses belongs with us," Maggie had shared with a sly smirk when we were walking into this meeting. "He's never going to know what hit him."

And he didn't. His dumbfounded look when we leave is one of flitting thoughts and desperation. He is out of a job, and he knows it.

"Once this goes public, he'll have a hard time getting a job taking orders, let alone giving them."

I admit it feels good, but it isn't over yet, and I am dreading the court appearance with Derrick and his family. Deciding it is time to go big or go home, I swallow my pride and fear of facing their inevitable disappointment by finally letting my parents and sister know about what is happening. It will be better coming from me before one of the other students from my high school catches wind of this and the rumors circle the campus. Mom would be pissed if she heard it from Sally, the gossip queen, and not from me.

They have me on speaker in the car after one of Laura's art shows, and the sound of the car accelerating at Mach speed isn't calming anyone's nerves.

"I'm glad I have you all on here at once," I say, thinking it will be much easier to just get it over with than to keep secrets. "Something has happened at school, over the last year with my ex. I wanted you all to hear it from me now that I've taken more action."

"Derrick is a tool," Laura chimes in, making me wish I had opted to just talk to Mom and Dad alone. "What did he do to you?"

Yep, she's smart.

"Thanks, Laura. That makes it easier." I sigh. "Yes, he wasn't a good boyfriend and he isn't a good guy overall. I filed for a restraining order and I've been in counseling. Yes, I'm okay, or will be, so don't worry."

"Did he hit you?" my dad growls.

"Yes," I reply boldly, shocking myself so much I nearly drop the phone. "But nothing like that will ever happen again, and I left him when I knew he wouldn't get help and didn't think he needed to."

What sounds like parts of the car meeting my dad's fist or feet causes Mom to shout out that she's going to stop the car to let him cool off. Knowing she is slowing down makes my breaths come in easier.

"I'm sorry if you are disappointed, and you must want to rip his head off, but I've done the right things. I have great people on my side and I'm safe. You taught me well. I found my resources and got the help I needed."

"But you didn't come to us," my mom cries to the backdrop of the hazard lights' rhythmic flickering. "Did you not think we could help you also?"

"Maybe if you hadn't kept her from having any fun or any experiences at all, this wouldn't have happened," Laura chimes in. "She isn't Rapunzel. I'm surprised you even let her go to Crimson."

121

Oh no. I can hear Mom's sobs before they even start.

"We did the best we could. We were just so scared about what could happen to her, I mean, to you, April," my mother mumbles quietly between sniffles. "We didn't live in a place where we had family around or close friends. You know your dad's work moved us out here. We didn't have a choice."

"Here we go again, blaming my work for everything."

"Guys, look, let's focus on the good, please. I am out of a crappy relationship, which will be the first and last one of its kind in my lifetime, and the fact that I got out and have taken the right steps shows how well you have raised me. No one is to blame."

"Except that dill-hole Derrick," Laura chirps in.

"Yes, I agree, and that's why I am going to court tomorrow to get the order settled."

"We'll be there first thing in the morning, or tonight if we need to," my mom spouts out. "What time do you have to be there?"

"No, please, don't take this the wrong way, but I don't want you to be there." My hands run through my hair, pulling it into a tighter ponytail than was already in place or I thought was humanly possible. "It isn't necessary. I-I don't want you to hear everything that way, but I promise I'll tell you. Just not this way. Please."

"Are you sure, sis?" Laura's serious tone is a rarity, so it catches me off guard. "You've done everything else on your own. You don't have to do this alone too."

"When did you get so mature?" I laugh.

"When Mom and Dad decided locking me down like you was impossible to do with *moi*." We all laugh at that one. Well maybe Dad not so much.

"It's your choice about tomorrow, sweetie, but you are coming home for spring break still, right?" My mom is obviously trying her hardest to ask instead of telling me. It seems Laura truly has broken them in over time.

"I have one stop before heading home, but yes, I'll be home for most if not all of the break."

Dad harrumphs in the background.

"It'll all be over soon, Dad. I think Derrick has gotten the picture," I assure.

"Well, you let me know if he doesn't." He snarls. "I can paint a clear one for him."

"Thanks, Dad."

The call ends with Mom's continuation of sniffles in the background and Laura telling Dad to have some faith in me. I guess I don't blame him. I kept this from them, from all of them, but I didn't even know what was really happening myself. If I had, I wouldn't be in this position. But since I didn't, I now have the power to make things better for someone else and for myself.

Chapter 13

Freedom

Staring at the woman behind Derrick makes me uneasy at first, but when she smiles back, I feel a weight lift away.

All of the horror stories of the guy getting a slap on the wrist, a tap on the head for his mistake, have been playing in my waking mind and dreams for days leading up to this court appearance. This is not that made-for-TV show or awful post on social media about the lack of justice for a woman, or man, that was on the other side of an injustice. No, things are going to change for Derrick, and from the looks of him, his downcast eyes darkened from lack of sleep, he is swallowing his pride and taking the punishment. Or maybe, just maybe, this is a picture of rock bottom, a time at which there is great change.

He doesn't fight the restraining order, instead turning to me and offering a side of himself I thought was long gone or never truly existed.

"I'm so sorry for all I have put you through. You were right, the whole time. I need to get help and I need to regroup and be the man I know I can be." He turns around to look at his parents for a breath before turning back to me. "And someone my parents will be proud of.

I've been only caring about myself and not about my actions. I hope someday you can forgive me."

My mouth opened at some point, but it wasn't so I could say anything; instead, it was forced open by the weight of his words. I almost smack myself to see if I need to wake from a dream.

"It takes a good deal of humility to admit when you are wrong and that you need to take more steps than you ever have before to improve yourself for the better." Judge Darlin doesn't smile when she speaks to Derrick, she only sets her gaze on him, perhaps even looking for the deception in the promise of better things. "Even though you show remorse and a willingness for change, and I know you have agreed to the schedule change to give Miss Mince her space, I will still be granting this restraining order."

The murmur behind Derrick is soft, not angry, but concerned.

"I know you may be worried about your record, Mr. Tinn, but you have to see it from my perspective and from Miss Mince's. An apology doesn't take away what has already been done."

Derrick nods in agreement and tries to give me a respectful smile.

"I also know that there are things that have come up about your past that may be to blame for what has continued this cycle for you, and with that, I hope you and your family can heal. I leave that information private in this hearing and leave it up to you to ever share on your own."

This statement startles me for a heartbeat, causing the rhythm to increase exponentially thinking of what may have happened to Derrick in his life to have created a monster out of the man standing not ten feet away from me.

It doesn't matter. You don't have to feel sorry for him.

But I can empathize. As I have thought many times, and what I've learned in class and group, the cycle can continue. Even when it's been such a horrific experience for a person, it can still somehow latch into the soul and psyche as the way things are and how they should be. It's a terrible unending circle without the right intervention. Maybe, now, Derrick's can be broken.

I turn to his parents, his dad pulling his wife in closer; they don't seem to show signs of being the guilty party, but possibly they knew or whatever occurred was definitely something they should have known? I close my eyes and will the tears to stay. He may have my empathy, but he won't see me cry ever again.

"Before I officially grant the restraining order to be in effect from now until one year from today, do you have anything to add, Miss Mince?"

My eyes slide to Derrick's. "I do hope you get the help that you need to heal and to change for the better. Perhaps in time I can forgive you, but for now, I just appreciate the responsibility you have taken and your willingness for change."

I nod and attempt to add a smile as well, but I can't. Instead, I shift my head to his mother and give her a hopeful smile. She returns it and mouths, *thank you*.

"I have to say, in all of my years, and in the times we've had brewing around us, I am pleasantly surprised and a little shocked with how maturely this has been handled by the Tinns and Miss Mince and her counsel.

In the past, this would have been ugly, full of denials and a parade of character witnesses, but this has given me hope for humanity as a whole."

Her eyes touch on each of us, ending on mine and holding them.

"For what you have gone through this past year, and for the lack of support on campus, I do hope this court has shown you that you have the support of the court and that you aren't alone." The all-business set to her eyes melts into a smile for a split second before regrouping into the awe-inspiring presence on the bench. "You are a brave young woman, Miss Mince. Don't ever forget that and know that you have done something extraordinary, not only for yourself, but for other victims of violence and abuse. I commend you and wish you the best."

"Thank you, Judge Darlin."

The hammering of the gavel should force me into motion, or at least to the side hug from Maggie, but it isn't until I see Derrick look at me one last time that I know it's really over. He may have lied to me before, but once I knew, I could always tell. This isn't an act. A broken man is before me, and most likely an older version of a little boy who endured his own form of abuse.

A weight lifts and I allow Maggie to usher me out of the courtroom, away from the building and into the sunlight. I stop on the steps, allowing my head to fall back while I soak in the springtime sun, its heat warming me from my cheeks down to my chest, where I swear my heart begins to pull itself back together, just a little, as if it mending its tears, chinks, and painfully gouged holes. All I needed was for it to start, and on its own, not due to another person loving me to help it repair. No, this slowly shifting work toward wholeness is something I have to do for myself.

But, even with the breaks, you love.

Yes, and now I've come this far on my own—well, not totally alone; I do have some amazing women in my corner—maybe I can find a way to sink into a glorious love. A real one that brings its own light to the other rips and pits in my heart. A love that I can trust, and that is with a man who is truthful, loyal, strong.

A hero and a protector?

Yes, words I can now use to define myself as well.

I've fidgeted with my hair in the rearview mirror long enough. It's time to head to the door and officially meet the woman who raised an incredible man, even despite having been abused and brought close to her death in an inferno, which took the life of her abuser instead.

A flicker to my right shifts my eyes from the world's worst mirror to the source of the motion. In a bright white linen shirt and a colorful yellow scarf wrapping her head, Shan's mom waves to me from the fenced-in backyard off in the distance. The hello changes to a summoning, so with a deep inhale and one fumble with my keys as I shove them into my purse, I am out the door. Sort of. My hip gets caught in the swinging motion of the darn thing closing, and I wince at the pain and at my klutzy car-exiting display.

Just friends, remember?

Yeah, yeah. Cool it.

I walk toward Ms. Bends at what feels like a slow-motion pace until I finally reach where she stands holding the gate open. I take a moment to look around to realize I don't see Shan's rental car in the driveway. I am a little early. I knew I should have texted him, but we confirmed last night. We haven't seen each other in nearly two weeks, only texting or talking a few times during our April-induced breakup. It wasn't easy, but it kept me focused, cleared my head, and brought me here. Who knows what would have happened, otherwise? Where my head was, it would probably have been on a collision course without hope of repair.

And now?

I'm here, aren't I?

"Hello, April," Shan's mom says while whipping something from her face with the back of her floral gardening glove. "Shan and his sister, Clara, had to run to the store. My forgetfulness got the best of me and I missed a couple items we *must* have for dinner. Come on back. The garden is showing off this year."

"Thank you, Ms. Bends."

"Please, call me Nicole."

"Yes. Thank you, Nicole." My feet are cemented on the other side of the fence. I can't move. For some reason, I'm stunned into a statue by being face to face with a woman whom I could see myself being if things hadn't changed for me.

But she's a survivor, so stop staring, you idiot.

"You have a lovely home," I manage, though my tongue wants to stay stuck to the roof of my mouth. "It's so peaceful here." The house, a white wood and stone cottage on a high hill more than an hour east of our campus, is both lovingly cared for and comfortably weathered.

Nicole holds the gate open and I step through, holding my cardigan sweater a little tighter in the cooling spring air. I almost wore a skirt but opted for jeans, aware of the change in elevation up here in the hills. The yellow of her scarf matches the little yellow lemons on my tank top, and I smile at our similarities and let go of my held breath at the agonizing ones that have kept me awake for many long nights.

Once I finally take in the backyard, the sprawling land lush with grass, flower beds, and a cement wall on the far end covered in vines, I smile for so many other reasons. This is her place of peace, and she deserves it. The life she has given to the garden reflects her new start from the ashes.

"Did you do this all yourself? It is breathtaking." It isn't an exaggeration. The sight causes me to touch my hand to my chest, which both clinches and releases in a lovely intensity. Beauty does this, beauty in the world, in music, in a dance, and in a touch. This place was created with love.

"Shan and I did most of the work, but Clara was here when we had to beat the crap out of the rocky ground to even begin to think of growing a thing in its stubborn dirt. I'll be sure to show you some before and after pictures, but you can get the general idea by looking over the wall. That's what this land was before it became the garden."

I follow her unfurling arm, a guide to the gorgeous array of snapdragons in all colors, daisies, and…that's about the extent of what I know I'm looking at. Thankfully, Nicole has placed little signs in various areas, and I walk around touching, reading, and admiring the sight and names of the colorful flowers, bushes, and grasses. They create levels and tell a story—one of rebirth from a rocky wreckage. This is Nicole's story now, and it is a display of strength and perseverance.

130

"I have some tea and water over here at the table. They should be back any minute, but I must be honest. I'm glad we have some time to ourselves."

My smile remains plastered to my face. I must look like a little girl in a candy shop. There is just so much to look at, and it doesn't stop at the plants. When we move toward the little mosaic table, we pass by two half barrels in the ground filled with water, plants, and goldfish in yellow, orange, white, and black, their tails flicking the surface while they gobble up the bugs venturing out to enjoy the warmer weather.

I find Nicole's eyes smiling in my direction.

"I'm glad you like it."

"I more than like it. It's like a fantasy world back here. You've created something magical." My eyes leave hers for only a moment to glance around again. "This must have taken a great deal of time and patience."

"Still does, but Shan comes up and helps me quite a bit. You should see me try to lug around the wheelbarrow full of mulch." She laughs. "The boy all but grounded me from trying that again."

"He's very helpful."

"You two have become close friends, I hear. Must be true if you've come up here to spend some time with us, away from your family."

"Yes, he's helped me through a tough time." My eyes drop. "Not that the difficulties are over, but I'm getting there."

"I heard about what you did, even after your school lacked the *cojones* to do anything for you."

This time I chuckle.

"You're a brave woman to keep going, and for not stopping even though Shan screwed things up along the way."

We reach the table and I sit down slowly, eyeing the strawberry-and-basil-infused water in the jar. Nicole reaches for the pitcher and pours me a glass, reading my desires by merely watching my body language. It's the training we've had in group as well. Ways to see the signs when words don't come outright, or to see through the lies. It's a talent, but at a cost.

"I hope you don't mind me bringing this up, but I know it would have been hard to talk about if I hadn't." Her hand moves absently to touch her scarf, assuring that it stays in place. "Even my closest friends never bring up the past, so I like to clear the air for people when the circumstances call for it. Ones like this."

"Your story, though I admit scared me, also moved me. And then, when I saw Shan…"

"Yes, that was quite a shock, I am sure," she adds.

"Quite, but Shan had seen me before, when I had, well, when I couldn't hide."

Her hand reaches out and touches mine, squeezing it softly and curling her fingers under my palm to take a gentle hold.

"I bring it all back for him, and I can't hurt him like that." I begin to hold her hand firmer, trying to use the supportive touch to get me through this. I don't even know what *this* is. "And you, I'm sure you'd rather your son be with someone more stable, less broken."

"Broken? I think not, young lady. And even so, even if there are spots crinkled and cracked, it's through those painful parts of our lives we find what we are made of, and what we can truly be. From what I hear, you are strong, brave, and bold. And though you'd

132

think he'd be biased, knowing how he feels about you, my son isn't one to falsely lay claims to someone's nature. He's never held back his true feelings, not especially when I stayed with his father when I should have left. It was my deaf ears that failed me and my family, but we can't stay stuck there, in that regret and failure. We have to move forward, through the chaos and the difficulty to find our brilliance." She motions around the garden, and I am in awe again as butterflies and dragonflies flit about, touching upon branches and lapping up nectar.

"I just need to be sure."

"Sure of what, dear?"

"Sure that I am clear of my mistake before I can open my heart again."

"That is a very sound way of thinking." She nods.

We sit in silence for a few minutes, looking around with broad smiles, enjoying the warm sunshine before shadows can begin to travel across the world Shan's mom has created with her family.

"Beauty out of the dirt and rocks," I remark.

"Yes. It's there, but it takes time and I won't lie, it's a lot of hard work. Ongoing work."

"Some things are worth it," I reply.

"Yes, they are."

I didn't hear the car come up the drive, or the gate swing open. It is the brightness on Nicole's face that signals Shan's arrival.

"I see that you two have officially met."

The melodic, masculine voice makes my heart quiver. In person he has a much stronger impact than on the phone—so much in fact that I doubt I can will my legs to stand with the shakiness he has created, or maybe it's more like a melting. Shan moves into my line of sight, taking my breath away in the golden rays of the coming sunset.

"Your mom's garden is unbelievable," I manage. "The work it must have taken you all."

"It was worth it." His words nearly echo mine exactly, making me wonder if he overheard me or if we are just that connected. I am opting to believe the latter.

So, not just friends?

Maybe not.

Dinner is outstanding. Many of the pickled veggies in the salad are from Nicole's garden, along with the lettuce. Her neighbors and friends have farms, so she gets local cheeses and meats as well. I can't remember when I felt this good after a meal.

Having always wanted to learn a little bit French, I enjoy learning from Clara, who's been living in France for over a year. Clara teases Shan constantly throughout the dinner while he struggles to pronounce the words in what she deems an appropriate accent, but I have a feeling he's lousing it up more drastically than is truly warranted.

"You're impossible," she grumbles to him on more than one occasion during the meal, though it's followed by her jesting tongue stuck out out in Shan's direction.

"You'd like my sister, Laura. You remind me of her." I laugh looking between the two. "Or maybe you two joking with each other reminds me of us."

"You're leaving to see her tonight? Is that right?" Clara asks. "It's going to be a dark ride—maybe you should just stay?"

It's Shan's turn to give her an annoyed look. "I'm sure April can make up her own mind. We are older than you, little sis."

But I am already considering the offer, not having thought it out very well with everything else going on.

Just friends time is officially out the door.

I giggle to myself only to have the heat flush my cheeks in front of Shan and his sister. Nicole just smiles between the exchanges, on occasion speaking perfect French with Clara, but most of the time simply enjoying having both of her kids home.

"Clara," Ms. Bends sings to her daughter, "why don't you help me clean up in the kitchen."

With a wink to her brother, Clara takes off after her mom with her dark ponytail bouncing along the way.

Now, with Clara and Nicole gone, Shan and I sit side by side, as we did all night, but now that low, buzzing spark between us flares to life.

"You can nearly see every star from up here," he declares, turning toward me with his dark eyes and brain-melting smile, sending a thrill through my chest.

"I'd love to see them. It's such a clear night." My response is shaky, and realizing that I'm not breathing, I take a fairly obvious inhale—shaky as well, of course.

"I'll tell my mom we're taking a drive. I have the perfect place." He stands, taking my hand with his to pull me to my feet as well. "Maybe grab a sweater?"

I nod as he pulls from me, letting his fingers go limp, but I don't release his hand.

"Your family is wonderful," I marvel softly, using his hand to pull him closer instead of letting him slip away. "I'm happy I came."

With a curve of his lips and a glimmer in his eyes, he takes my words and motions to mean exactly what I hope he'd notice. My idea of just being friends was just that, an idea, and one I have decided to cast aside after nearly two weeks of distance.

I lift to my toes as his head dips down. My lips, nearly touching his, tingle with a vibration, with a need. I move in that last half an inch and meet his mouth with mine. It may not have been the deepest, longest kiss, but it was the most passionate one. One without the worries of my past, or his.

"I'm guessing you've changed your mind?"

"How'd you guess?" I smirk.

"That was not something I've ever felt, or done, with just a friend," he replies while brushing the back of his hand against my cheek. "And I may not have known you for long, but I do know you, April, and that was more than just a kiss."

I heat at his words but ignore my potential for shyness and press my palms to his chest. "You are very perceptive. Of course, I knew that about you. It's one of the things I love about you."

Shan's eyes widen and his chest lifts before I have a chance to move my hand over it to circle his shoulders.

"Weren't we going somewhere?"

Shan's head nods. He's at a loss for words. My worry that I may have said too much is pushed aside by the surety in my heart that he feels the same way.

With a blanket, desserts, and few of his mom's bottles of beer, Shan and I set off to get a better look at the stars. By the looks of his path, we are going to a very private place, and the anticipation is bringing titillating pictures of what may happen tonight to my mind.

"I found this spot looking for a good jogging route. I think you'll like it."

We left the paved road a while ago, but I hardly notice the bouncing as I take in the beauty, even in the dark where the moonlight hits the trees and nighttime bloomers. After Shan stops the car where we can no longer go farther once our headlights meet a wall of trees, he points to a trail off to the right.

"It's a short walk to the clearing. It has a killer view."

While I close the car door behind me, Shan wrestles in the trunk. Side by side, we follow the wide beam of his flashlight. Once the trail begins to tighten, I snag the bulky blanket under his other arm and follow his back the rest of the way.

"You weren't kidding," I manage, once the curtain of trees parts to reveal the spectacular view.

The world unfolds both below us and above. My eyes shift from the town beneath to the mountains in the distance, and then over to where I watch as Shan shakes out the blanket before I look upward to the blanket of stars in the sky.

"So many heroes and their magical creatures, families, and nemeses," I observe.

"Yes, I think you're going to have to put yourself up there someday."

"You'll be up there with me. Which ones should be ours? They can't all be taken yet, can they?" I smile at Orion's Belt, the constellation I'm drawn to in the night sky ever since I was a child. "My aunt loves the stars. We always look for Orion, Perseus, Andromeda, and Pegasus. Now, when I look at Orion, I'll think of you."

With a pat on the quilted blanket, Shan draws my attention to his left. My trembling legs make it difficult to sit gracefully, but I somehow manage to snuggle up next to him, both our gazes cast to the glowing lights in the sky.

"I don't have any star people in my family, but I do know the Big Dipper and the Little Dipper," he admits. "And I love the movie *Clash of the Titans,* so I at least know who you're talking about. Can you see them now?"

"Yes, just over there Perseus, Andromeda, and Cassiopeia are in a line, but I can't see Pegasus tonight. Sometimes I can find a wingtip." The four constellations cluster together, the mom, the daughter, and the hero with his winged beauty, and I wonder again where our story will go. "You know"—I smirk— "I made a *Clash of the Titans* board game in middle school. Medusa was my favorite baddie."

"She used to give me nightmares," Shan admits. "My mom said I woke her up every night for weeks after seeing her in that movie."

Our gazes shift upward again, our eyes roaming a sky full of heroes and villains, all Greek myths alight in a pitch-dark sky. The rhythms of the surrounding forest create a soundtrack to this beautiful night, the perfect backdrop to a happier story down on Earth than many of the tragedies in the sky.

"Two heroes together up in the stars. I like it, though it's still sometimes hard to think of myself in that way." My statement is a whisper since my breath has been taken away by the sight of the man next to me in the cascading night. His snug, light-weight jacket reveals his strength while his soft, dark eyes and light shadow of a beard exude a sexiness I won't resist for long.

"What's not to see? I see a champion for women who can't speak for themselves. That's what we called

138

my mom once she started doing her talks, and I think it rings true for you too."

It's still hard to think of myself as a hero after what I allowed to happen. Is there really a fine line between strengths and weaknesses?

I can't peel my eyes away from Shan and the view of stars reflected in his eyes. He smiles warmly, and I know in this moment I could never have stayed away and just been friends for that long anyhow.

"Thank you for giving me the space when I needed it."

"Yeah, that wasn't easy. I was hopeful, and now here you are with me tonight."

"The power of positive thinking," I declare.

Shan chuckles and then leans in, his hand moving into my hair before pressing his lips to mine while finding a way to weave between them with his tongue. I find his with mine and we both begin a sort of dance around each other. Both of us kissing and touching and moving our hands back and forth between each other's hair, back, legs, and then when he finds my chest, I push against him even more.

The privacy underneath the evening sky makes it easy for me to pull my shirt up over my head and slowly unclasp my bra. Shan watches me with wonderment. As if on autopilot, he removes his shirt as well. While we face each other, both of us on our knees, I take a moment to touch each part of his chest, along his ribs, down to his firm stomach, and back up to his shoulders. With both perfectly built shoulders in my hands, I release one to smoothly reach up his neck and grab Shan to kiss him. He uses his momentum to push me down onto my back. Leveraging himself to hover on top of me, while sending soft fingers down my neck, between my breasts, and without dwelling there for long, he reaches one hand to unzip my pants just enough for him to be able to reach down inside. I go tense and then limp in a matter of seconds. My mind obviously does not know what to do once he has ahold of my being. My very essence drips from my body and exhales from my lungs. This is bliss.

I pant as his fingers slide in and out of me, first one and then another. His mouth closes around mine with a moan. I try to squirm beneath him to get my hand to the top of his jeans. With a flick of two fingers the top button gives way, but I can't reach the zipper. A dizziness takes over and my arm goes slack as his rhythm inside me continues, but I manage to get ahold of myself and snag behind his neck to look into his eyes. He stops for a moment, lowering to kiss me again, and I manage to get my hand to his zipper and push it down. I try to work to remove his jeans, but Shan thankfully lifts off of me, coming to stand before dropping his jeans and boxers to the blanket. I shimmy and deftly work my hands and remove everything else, tossing it aside.

At first, a chill pours through me from the cold air, but it quickly changes to one of building anticipation. I long for him to be inside of me, but instead of freezing for a split second once he lowers on top of me once again, my body responds to something deep inside my mind.

He's not Derrick. He'll never be him either.

"Are you sure this is okay? We can slow down if you want." He senses my unease. Stupid subconscious.

"No, please don't stop. I want this, I really do. It's just…"

"I'm not like him, April. I would never hurt you like he did, I promise."

"You don't even have to say anything. I knew that a long time ago."

A slow pressure touches me, delicately searching and rubbing along my soft skin where I am already stimulated to the brink. I take slow inhales and he gives me a sexy kiss before mimicking my deep breaths.

Once he enters me, it is a blissful heat and pressure. Something more than physical passes between us as we make love, and I am lost in this moment, surrounded by a beautiful backdrop of the forest and night sky. The stars above dance to our passion along with the creation of a bond stronger than anything I have ever experienced before. This is love and true passion, and it is new and incredible. As if it was hiding inside all along, and Shan is the only one who could have fully set it free. We share the climbing and aching build-up before our sensual tandem releases.

Shan's hand curls the side of the blanket around us and we lie side by side, reveling in the passion and bliss as if we were the only two people in the world. "You are amazing, April. I have never felt this way before. I don't want this night to end."

"I think it will live on in my heart forever, plus we have all of the time in the world together now." I sigh while curling into his chest. "Nothing or no one will keep us apart ever again."

"I wish I could teach him a lesson, but I know that will only cause more problems for us. I learned that the hard way with my dad."

"I think he's learned one already, and I really am sorry about your mom, and sorry for all of you. I can't even imagine what you've gone through, what you're

141

still going through, but you three have each other. He could never destroy that bond or your love for each other."

"It's helped me see what love isn't, and now I know what true love is. It's how I feel for you." Shan's fingers lift my chin to look into my eyes.

"You do? I, I think I've been in love with you since before we even spoke. That's silly isn't it?"

"No, April. I love you, silly, happy, sad, and all."

"I love you, too."

"You are perfect for me, and you look unbelievably gorgeous and sexy tonight," he purrs into my ear. "I'm sorry if I can't take my hands off of you."

"And I don't want you to."

Chapter 14

Chasing

I wake in the darkness of Shan's room. Shan's breathing nearly lulls me back to sleep, but it's a rare morning when I wake and manage to find dreamland once again. We must have fallen asleep in here even though his mom had already set up a bed for him on the couch. I don't want to break her rules in her own home within the first twenty-four hours of knowing her, so I plan my departure from the room. I'm sure that would be a record somewhere. It was hard to separate after our first time making love, but that won't be the excuse I give to anyone but Shan.

Slowly, and with only a *shoosh* of sound from the sheets, I roll off the bed into a silent crouch. The tips of my toes pad along the carpet. I snag my running shoes and an outfit from my bag and slip into the bathroom.

Shan's trail to see the stars is part of his favorite running loop. I memorized it on the way back to the house, managing to focus on something other than what had unfolded on the blanket underneath a glowing, evening sky. The moon had brightened to a broad beam of light, which made it easy to see the path, so I know I can follow it even with the sun at least an hour away from rising. I can't sleep now anyhow, so I might as well get my run in.

After changing and lacing up my shoes, my rubber soles sneak back to my purse where I grab my phone and kitty knuckles. I may be brave, but I'm not stupid—though I doubt anyone else will be up and about, except for some nocturnal critters who are crawling back home for their bedtime.

The air is brisk, much cooler than when I was in Shan's arms. When I reach the split to pick the six-mile or three-mile loop, I opt for the shorter one. My legs may or may not be a little shaky after last night's activities. Tingles shoot through me at the thought of my body being pressed against Shan's. Pictures of new places and ways I can feel him again before I leave today take my attention from the trail and I nearly bite it tripping over a root.

Steady there. You seem distracted for some reason. Snort

Real funny.

I move on, my gait becoming smooth like swimming through water. The ground moves quickly below me, and I eat away a good two and a half miles before I lose focus again and find the previous root's best friend. I catch myself once again before I can bust my knees and hands on the ground, though my shoe slips off my heel, bringing me to a halt.

When I bend down, my hair tie floats to the ground, having snapped at some weak link, freeing the mass of winding curls into my face. I blow a few strands away long enough to create somewhat of an opening in my sight to slip on and re-tie my shoe.

"This is going well," I whisper to the trees. Despite always having an extra hair tie on my wrist, I am ill-prepared this fine morning.

This is night, not morning.

Okay, so maybe 4:00 a.m. is a little early, but the moon makes it bright enough for one to think dawn is breaking over the horizon. Using my fingers to twist and twirl my hair, I manage to tie it onto itself into a braided knot. Now to see if it'll survive the bounce of my stride over the uneven ground.

Before I can move back into action, the *thunking* echo of a car door slamming melds my shoes to the dirt. Hands to my jacket pockets, I slip my fingers into my kitty spikes of pain and focus my eyes all around me. The six-mile loop area merges into this path up ahead, and on the other side of that must me the road. What I had thought was the glow of the moon through the thicket to my right disappears in a blink. I swallow hard at the realization that it was a shine of a headlight and not the glowing beams of nighttime's sun.

Metal groans and shuffling follows. I crouch low, moving slowly to hide behind a trunk of a tree close to where the Houdini light had flickered away. A grumbling voice trickles spikes of pointy feet down each vertebra.

It's probably another runner, or maybe a hunter. You better get your booty back fast.

I ignore her, me, and lean forward enough to spot a figure dipping in and out of the trunk of an old, large sedan. The glow of a light follows the cursing and then a sloshing hum. I spy two rectangular containers that the person places on the ground next to his car.

Gas cans.

I swallow, or at least try to, when the trunk closes with a thud and the beam of light hits the face of the suspicious person in the dark.

Is that…

It is. I'd remember that face anywhere. After poring over article after article on the Carp family tragedy, that face woke me more than once from a nightmare—John Carp, Shan's dad.

How? He's dead.

But I don't wait to answer. Legs and arms pump harder than I ever thought possible as I bolt back to Nicole's house. I ignore the pain in my chest and calves, driving ahead. I need to warn them, I need to save them, but I am also gambling here. What if my thought that he's walking the rest of the way is wrong? What if he jumps in the car with those full cans of gas snuggled next to him in the front seat? I'll never beat him.

It makes the most sense that he's walking. Just keep moving.

My lungs burn, the cold air rushing in fast and hard. Maybe I should have tried to take him down alone, or as least brought my phone and called the police.

No service out here, remember.

I do. Shan and I realized that when we tried to open a star chart app last night. Pushing the doubt away, I focus instead on tearing apart that last half mile and saving the man I love and his family. Unraveling from its knot, my hair flies behind me, staying out of my eyes as if it knows the seriousness of this situation and to butt the hell out. My feet hit pavement as I exit the trail, and I take a quick peek behind me—no one yet.

I pass houses in a blur, pushing off my toes as I take the hill to the house. It finally comes into view, and I nearly break down crying. I've made it. I beat him here. Now what?

Move.

Those last few steps seem to take forever as I lurch to the door, trying the knob first before remembering that I locked it behind me, The hide-a-key is around back, but I can't waste time, so my mind clicks to raise my fist and bang like a crazy person on the door. Before I can make a sound upon the distressed wood, someone grabs me from behind, one hand in my hair and one over my mouth while I am pulled away from both my safety and my warning to the others.

"You made me drop my cans when I heard you take off from the woods," the masculine voice hisses in my ear. "You don't know these trails like I do, missy. I caught up with you quick." The suffocating heat from Shan's father's breath makes my head swim in disgust.

I try to go limp, hoping I'll catch John off guard and he'll drop me, but he hangs on tight. I've managed to hide my other hand in my jacket pocket, forcing the metal from my knuckles to dig into my flesh with the tightness of my grip.

"You think you can get away from me that easily? Sorry to break it to you, young lady, but you're coming back this way nice and slow." He's dragging me, despite my back-kicks and thrashing limbs. "Now cut that out. I have ways to keep you still while I finish what I started years ago. But I'm guessing you know that already, don't you? You're my boy's little whore now. I hope he's gotten all of my messages."

The paint, the fire—it was him all along. A man back from the dead who has found his family in their new home away from the people in the town who failed them and, apparently, also failed to identify the

147

remains. Perhaps those loyal to him took the truth to his grave. A racing mind moves my lips, and I mumble these truths through his hand, but John doesn't loosen his hold. I kick and flail, but Shan's dad is a sizable man, even bigger than his son and hell-bent on rage and revenge. It can't end like this, not after everything Shan and his family have gone through and not after my escape from a potentially similar future.

The training from self-defense class kicks into drive, and I prepare. This time, instead of dropping, I tip forward before pushing off the balls of my feet and jumping backwards. Along with that motion, I find a way to move my mouth enough to bare my teeth and bite down on his fingers. Mr. Carp stumbles enough for me to turn around, kitty in hand, and swing into the softness of his stomach. The pointed ears of pain dive into flesh like a spoon into thick yogurt while I use my other hand to crack up into his nose before I make a swift, stumbling retreat. I hit the ground more than once, forced to crab walk backward, the fear and adrenaline leaving my brain dead for a moment, but then I wake up and find my bearings just before I unleash a torturous wail.

"*Help*! *Shan*, anyone. *Help*!" My screams echo in the hillside.

Dogs begin to bark in an instant, their sharp howls into the night so haunting that even my attacker halts his progression. Blood drips from where one hand holds his nose while the other clutches his stomach.

"You little bitch. You stabbed me. And I think you broke my nose."

"That's right, you son of a bitch. Stay away from me and this family."

"It's my family. Mine! And that whore in there is going to pay for taking it from me. She should be dead!"

"Speak for yourself, Dad."

Like a whip, my head turns toward the sound of Shan's voice. The cadence and promise of safety give me the push I need to flip over my body and will myself to stand. My feet slip on the gravel as I'm yanked back by my ankle. Carp senior has me again.

"Let her go!"

"Drop the gun first, son, and I will," John sneers to Shan while using both hands now to force me toward him before turning me around to face Shan while in his clutches. This time the sight of the gun in undeniable. "You don't want to kill your old man, do you? Not again, that is."

"Maybe this time it'll stick." A click of what I assume is the safety makes me jump. The gun is raised in our direction but aimed at his dad.

He could miss.

"Don't accidentally hit this little beauty."

"Shan…" I cry. I don't want him to kill anyone, but I don't want his dad to go free either.

Lights come on in the houses scattered about, but the lots are far-spreading, and I can't tell if anyone is peering out of their windows. Shan's mom or sister must have called the police by now, right? How long will it take them in this slow, little town of foothills and gardens?

My eyes spy my kitty knuckles in the gravel and dirt a few feet away, but John has me in a tight hold, so close to his chest that the slow trickle of blood from his nose drips into my hair. Realizing I am looking around and readying to escape again, John wraps his fingers

149

around my neck, squeezing one tick at a time. Air struggles to find its way to my lungs, and I imagine the raspy sounds of Nicole's damaged windpipe voice that was created at the hands of the same man who holds my own.

"You're hurting her. Let her go, John." Nicole's voice is no longer in my imagination, instead coming to life on the porch next to her son. "Haven't you done enough? When will it end?"

"When you are dead, Nicole. This is all your fault. You and the boy. I'll take you both this time. Oh, and this little doe for the fun of it."

Sirens sound in the distance, but his grip doesn't weaken.

"It's over, John. The police are coming," Shan warns, moving slowly off the porch.

"Watch it. Don't come any closer or I'll snap her neck."

Shan freezes. I think he hopes John will make a run for it, but it seems like he's planning to go down in a different blaze of glory and take me with him. Stars dance in my vision and a new darkness encroaches as the peaks of dawn flame to life.

"Dad. Oh God, Dad, no." Cara has joined her family, with eyes darting from her dad's face to the grip he has around my neck. Her body begins to vibrate in what I can only guess is fear. "I thought you were dead."

My eyes flutter, closing so that I can't see her any longer while a roar bubbling up in my ears takes away my ability to hear a response.

Am I dying? I can't breathe and none of my senses are working right.

This can't be how I will die. Twenty and at the hands of an abuser, when I stood against my own, and in front of the man I love.

Noises manage to break into the rush of blood in my ears; they must be voices, and then I'm falling, my face hitting the hard gravel with nothing to stop my plight. A deep raking breath burns my lungs and scorches like alcohol has been set on fire in my throat. My eyelids grate as if sandpaper has taken their place. I slowly blink them open to see Shan's gun on the ground and his feet come into view.

"You made a smart choice. Now, sweetheart, bring the gun to Daddy."

God no, I thought it was over, but Shan has just given him what he wanted by dropping his gun.

"By the barrel, not near the trigger, there you go," he coaxes to Cara. "Hand it over."

Something takes over me, a force of nature or perhaps my other voice creating a more physical presence. Whatever it is, I sense my brass knuckles under my chest and slide my arm underneath my body to get ahold of them again. Shan's eyes peer into mine where he's crouched in front of me. He doesn't try to stop me or help me up; instead, something silent and calculating passes between us. Even though my energy is surging, I mock weakness as I let Shan help me to my feet. John's vicious laughter at the display only fuels me further.

A blink, or a breath, maybe it's just a twist of my feet on my toes that passes. Whatever it is, it's fast, and in that flutter of time I lunge at John. I feign a dive at his stomach, knowing he'll overreact at his injury and try to block me before piercing him in his shoulder. The man screams and thrashes about, but I manage to

151

remove my weapon from a now overflowing wound and back away as Shan rushes in and tackles his dad to the ground. Hands grab my shoulders to pull me away, but I can't leave Shan as he tries to pin his father to the ground.

Cara tosses the gun away from the fight, the sounds of sirens and the strobe light of blue, white, and red flashing to life around us. Two cars pull up behind us, skidding to a halt, sending pebbles flying at us like a hailstorm.

"Police! Everyone stay calm." The female voice is stern but wary. "Move to the house, ladies. Keep your hands where we can see them." The officer approaches us cautiously with her gun drawn but down. Her eyes focus on the blood dripping from my hands.

"Help him," I screech, pointing at the fight between father and son. "His father is trying to kill us."

Two more officers creep toward the bodies in battle with weapons drawn. "John Carp, sir, we know who you are, and we need you to stand down. Let's not make things worse. Get up nice and slow with your hands on your head."

But John isn't listening.

Shan manages to get free, kicking his dad in the stomach before creating space to let the officers deal with his father.

"We aren't in your town anymore, Dad. You won't get away with it this time." Shan continues to back up, reaching behind for my hand.

Once we touch, we move back toward his mom and sister, forming a united front. Stunned and beaten, but together.

Shan's father looks from us to the officers with a face like that of a mad dog's, frightened and crazed.

He's not going to stop.

With a howl, John dives for the gun Cara tossed away, but before he can grab ahold of the hammer, the officer next to us fires a shot, hitting Shan's dad in the back of the leg.

"That's your only warning. Now get your hands on your head!"

With a growl, John gets to his knees, hands following slowly while he turns his bloodied face to look at us. Rage shadows his face and a flicker of something I can't place runs through the glaze of his eyes.

"Hands, now!"

John turns in a flash, charging after the two officers like a maddened wraith in the night. A haunting eruption of gunfire and dogs howling brings the nightmare to an end—for good this time.

Epilogue

A New Page

This is what normal feels like. Hand in hand, walking across campus with warm sunshine on our faces instead of a constant tracking over our shoulders.

We keep our slow pace with arms swinging. Shan and I have completed our finals, now officially finished with our second year. Now, summer approaches with internships and free time to spend with each other. Travel and living a normal life away from the stressors of our past will be our shared futures, ones we both look forward to as the school year comes to a close.

Shan, now officially Shan Bends, joined his sister and mother in changing his last name to his mother's maiden name. My boyfriend, officially since our *just friends* zone ended over the spring break we'll never forget, made the decision in hopes of closing the door to a past he'd rather forget. Forget? Never. And to forgive? Impossible, but time and love can lessen the memory. Yet those painful parts of his past will be shoved aside, replaced by ones of caring, of loving me, and with a life lived without the evils of his past.

The birds, now releasing their babies from the springtime nests to learn on their own, fill the campus with sounds. Only a few others walk around with us; the other students are either completing finals or at the end-of-year celebrations in town. Neither Shan nor I will be joining our friends and roommates; instead, we walk hand in hand, opting to explore one of the trails around campus while we prepare to meet our families for dinner in the city.

"You don't have to be nervous. I know my family will love you." My smile is in tandem with a squeeze to his hand.

"Oh, yeah?" he asks while coming to a stop and pulling me into his arms. "How do you know that?"

"Because I love you. And because they know what you've done for me and that you have and will take care of me."

"Always," he promises, and seals it with a kiss.

We are surrounded by the sounds of summer. Chirps, rustles, and scurries fill the air with life. My life, Shan's life, our lives, and we spend them together.

"Always," I repeat before we kiss again, holding each other in the freedom of a future of our own making.

There's nothing to trap us, and we have each other to protect our hearts from now on.

THANK YOU FOR READING
A Protector's Touch

The Alex Conner Chronicles
(Urban Fantasy/Supernatural Suspense)
Trust: The Alex Conner Chronicles Book One
Truth: The Alex Conner Chronicles Book Two
Forbidden: An Alex Conner Chronicles Novella
Only: The Alex Conner Chronicles Book Three

Eve of the Exceptionals
(YA Epic Fantasy)

The Dark Angel Series
(Dark Urban Fantasy)
A Darker Fall: A Dark Angel Novella

Jake the Growling Dog
(A Children's Picture Book about Kindness, Diversity,
& Friendship) under the pen name Samantha Shannon.
Jakethegrowlingdog.com; @jakethegrowlingdog

KEEP UP WITH PARKER SINCLAIR

Webpage: *www.parkersinclair.net*
Amazon Author Page: *https://www.amazon.com/Parker-*

Sinclair/e/B00Q33GTQM
Facebook Fan Page: *www.facebook.com/ParkerSinclairbooks/*

Instagram: *@ParkerSinclairauthor*
Twitter: *@Parker_Sinclair*
Join my newsletter for free fantasy/Sci-Fi books:
http://eepurl.com/b9q07X